Extreme Circumstances

A novel

By
Cereka Cook

RJ Publications, LLC

Newark, New Jersey

The characters and events in this book are fictitious. Any resemblance to actual persons, living or dead, is purely coincidental.

RJ Publications
Cmonet_@hotmail.com
www.rjpublications.com
Copyright © 2007 by Cereka Cook
All Rights Reserved
ISBN 0-9769277-6-4

Printed in Canada

March 2007

11 12 13 14 15 16 17 18 19 20

Acknowledgements

First, I would like to thank my parents Jesse Martin Jr. and Linda McCleskey. Thank you for always believing in me and loving me...*the limit is no longer the sky.*

Clinton McCleskey, Dr. Louis Anderson, Darryn Hardy, Lionel Hemmons, Reginald Williams, Deborah Harris-Johnson, Nigel Barnes and Carlos Traylor thank you all for being so supportive.

Ladaria Smith—thanks, cuz, for always giving me some inspiration to continue to write even when I got stumped....'preciate ya.

Chad A.Rayner...good lookin' out. You always had my back since day one even before I wrote one word, you always told me I could do it. And I know I got on your nerves when I asked you to read each chapter in progress. Gotta love me! (smile)

To the rest of the family and extended family...Tynisia Hanson, Steven Hanson, Jeffery Cook, AJ Manning, Gloria Cook, Marshall Cook, Michael Cook, Stacey Campbell, Craig Knighten, Kesha Fortune-Haynie, Vince Haynie, Stacy Rumsey-Patrick, Melvin Patrick, Ron Weeks and Julia Weeks.

Oyin Jones-thanks for the Chi-town info and for giving me a sense of fashion. Toni Jackson-thanks Tete! Thanks for looking out for me and supporting me like a mother/big sister. Ingrid Judge-thanks for telling everybody you could think of about 'Extreme Circumstances'.

Last but not least, to the RJ Publications family. Rich, (Richard Jeanty), thank you for giving me a chance to get my name out there, and not taking me through unnecessary drama. I'm ready to create several number one best sellers!! And to the editor, Nancy Rousseau, thank you for smoothing things out for me.

And a special thanks to Keith Saunders for making the bomb-ass book covers!

~sometimes fiction isn't far from the truth~

Chapter 1

As Chanel is driving to meet Donnell she thinks about what she's going to say to him. After all, she and Donnell have been doing, whatever it is they're doing for about five years now and at twenty-eight years old and in love with Donnell, she's definitely ready for marriage and he ought to be, too.

Chanel's thoughts were abruptly interrupted by her cell phone. She looked at the caller ID and noticed it was her best friend, Janai.

"What's up, girl?" she said.

"Whaddup, cow?" Janai said with a thick New York accent.

"Nothing, just meeting Donnell for dinner. What are you up to?"

"Oh, well never mind then. I was calling to see if you wanted to go to Crickets tonight. It's karaoke night."

"Sorry. Count me out tonight. We can go tomorrow or next week sometime, because right now I'm going to see my man," Chanel boasted.

"Yeah, yeah." Janai rolled her eyes. She couldn't stand Donnell. She felt that he was transparent and couldn't understand why her best friend couldn't see what she saw. She felt that Chanel deserved better.

"So anyway, where are you guys meeting?"

"Showcase Eatery."

"Where's that?"

"It's over on Old National. You know, over by the police station."

"They got good food?"

"Best on the south side."

"Word? Then I might have to check that out one day. I'll get one of these nigga's to take me since Jordan's ass is always broke."

"Girl, you need to give that man a break. He's a hard working brotha that makes an honest living *and* he's paying your damn rent."

"Whatever! If he's so good then you take his ass. Besides he needs to be payin' my damn rent. He's I' all my goods."

Chanel shook her head. Janai was indeed her best friend, but Chanel didn't always agree with her. "Janai, I got to go. I'll talk to you later. Peace!"

Chanel walks through the lobby and spots Donnell in a secluded area of the restaurant. He looks so damn good, she thought! Dayum!!

His back was facing her but she could see he had on a nice loose fitting pair of jeans with an orange colored pullover shirt that accentuated his gorgeous, chocolate skin.

She quickly ducked into the bathroom to check herself out to make sure she looked drop-dead gorgeous when he laid eyes on her. She looked through her purse and found her chestnut lip pencil and her lip-gloss. She applied just enough to accentuate her natural beauty. Donnell always talked about how sexy he thought her lips were.

7

People were always telling Chanel that she looked like a dark-skinned, Sanaa Lathan. But humph, she thought. *Sanaa ain't got nothing on me. Because I'm the shiznit!* Chanel laughed at her own thoughts. She had on a v-neck periwinkle stretch blouse and a black skirt with a thigh high split and a pair of black sandals. *I know I look good*, she thought to herself. She checked her face one more time then she finger-combed her spirals and walked out of the bathroom towards the table. Chanel walked up behind Donnell and tenderly nibbled his earlobe.

"Hey sexy chocolate man," she said in a sexy lowered voice.

Donnell stood up and embraced Chanel and gave her a quick kiss on the lips. His six-two stature complimented her one hundred-thirty pound frame.

"No, you're the sexy one, Chanel." He noticed the split in her skirt as she was sitting in her chair. "Girl, you have the sexiest legs I have ever seen." He took her by the hand to twirl her around. "Stand up a minute. Let me check you out."

Chanel blushed. As she stood up she felt a little embarrassed because she noticed that people were starting to stare at the two of them.

"Now turn around…"

"Donnell!"

"Aw, you know you like it," Donnell told her rather confidently.

Chanel smiled. And as she was sitting down the waitress approached their table. Donnell ordered a beer to go with his meal. He couldn't stand fruity drinks. Chanel on the other hand loved fruity drinks, but decided on a semi-sweet wine. As they waited for their dinner they conversed about their jobs. Donnell enjoys web design and programming (working from home), but has just been recently offered a six figure opportunity of a lifetime for a major corporation. He just can't stand the bullshit politics of corporate America.

As for Chanel, Atlanta had been good to her as well. Working in the control room at Fox-5 news has been everything she could have imagined. It's exciting and challenging and she loves it.

The two had been enjoying their evening until Chanel suddenly changes the subject.

"Do you remember the first time we met back home?"

Oh shit, Donnell thought. *Every time she reminisces it always comes to us discussing the state of our relationship.*

"Of course I do," he replied with a half-hearted smile. "I told you when you came down that escalator and I saw those legs and that chocolate skin and that smile I have to admit, you had a brotha hypnotized, mesmerized….all that shit."

Chanel smiled. "Well, I'm just glad I ended up missing my flight that day, otherwise we might not have met."

"You never know. Things do happen for a reason."

"Well if you really believe that, then what is our purpose? I mean if you were so mesmerized, why have we not moved on to the next level? You know how I feel about you and where I want this relationship to go."

Oh God, I knew she was going to start this shit. "Chanel, I told you that I'm just not ready to settle down yet. I'm just enjoying my freedom."

Yeah right! Freedom is just another word for player, and that's exactly what Donnell was.

"Donnell, you're thirty-four. When are you going to grow up? By now you should want to settle down and have a family."

That was the furthest thing from his mind. "Why? Because that's what you want, Chanel?"

She looked at him and tightened her lips and flared her nostrils.

Donnell became more evasive and tried to change the subject. "See this is exactly what I didn't want to happen. Baby, let's just enjoy each other's company right now and talk about this another time, okay? Come on please; just let it drop for a moment."

Chanel was about to rip Donnell a new one, but by this time the waitress had come back with their meals.

"Will you be needing anything thing else at the moment?" the waitress asked.

Donnell just looked down at his plate and flexed his jaws. Then he took the last swig of his beer.

Chanel was so upset she had lost her appetite and asked the waitress to bring her a box to take the rest of the food home, while Donnell asked her to bring him the check. The two of them said nothing to each other. She just grabbed her purse and walked toward the parking lot when Donnell was still paying for the food. He noticed her walking off and yelled, "Chanel wait!"

She didn't look back. She just headed for her car. Donnell ran after her. He knew he could smooth things over with her. He always did. Donnell was so smooth and charming he could talk an Eskimo into buying ice. Besides, he was horny and he was damn sure going to get him some ass that night. When he caught up with her, she was just about to get in her car. He noticed that she had begun to tear up. He pushed her hair out of the way and kissed her forehead.

"Chanel let's just go back to your place. We can sip on some wine, I'll massage your feet, we can get in the hot tub...."

She nodded. Chanel understood exactly what Donnell meant. It was the fastest drive to her home. The anticipation of Donnell's pleasure island kept Chanel's foot on the accelerator like she was trying to win a NASCAR race. Once they arrived they headed for the elevator. Chanel lived in a high rise condominium on the top floor.

Once they were inside the elevator, Donnell grabbed Chanel by her waist. He wanted her right there in the elevator. He sensed she wanted the same thing, too.

Donnell looked over to his left at Chanel and reached for her face and gently slid his tongue in her mouth and their tongues seemed as if they were playing ring-around-the –rosy. Chanel slowly caressed Donnell's crotch as he kissed her. She could feel that he was rock hard. She wanted him inside her *right now*! She was on *fire*! He slid his hand in between the split on her skirt and pulled her panties down far enough to feel her juices flowing. He massaged her womanhood gently.

"Oh, Donnell," she sighed.

Chanel's moans were driving Donnell crazy. He had to have her. He had always fantasized about having hot sex in an elevator. Now was a good time to turn his fantasy into a reality.

He pressed the emergency stop button. The elevator halted. He continued to slide her panties all the way down. Chanel lifted each leg so Donnell could get the panties off completely. Donnell pinned Chanel against the wall of the elevator. He stooped down and placed each of Chanel's legs behind his head enabling his face to be level with her sweet spot.

He playfully licked her clitoris with his tongue. Round and round, up and down, faster then slower. Chanel moaned with delight. She felt as if she were in a whirlwind of pleasure. Each lick brought her to brand new heights of ecstasy.

Chanel swiveled her hips to the motion of his tongue. Grabbing his head and pulling him deeper and deeper inside her.

Donnell moved his tongue slower this time to sort of tease her until she finally climaxed and he drank all her love juices.

She panted. "Ooh, damn you know you make me feel so good!"

He looked up at her and smiled. He got up wiping his mouth and nose. "I love to watch you cum," he told her.

He pressed the elevator emergency button again. This time to release it and the elevator continued to climb up. They finally reached the third floor and walked toward Chanel's place.

Chanel's condo consisted of three bedrooms and two full bathrooms. One of the extra bedrooms she used as a guest room. The other, was used as an office. She also had a full deck with a built-in Jacuzzi. She locked the door behind her and Donnell reached and pulled her to him again and kissed her deeply. He reached with his right hand to pull her panties down and remembered he took them off on the elevator.

They both looked down, then looked up at each other and laughed once they realized that Chanel left her panties on the elevator.

Donnell wanted to pick up where they left off, but Chanel wanted to slow things down a bit. "Baby, let's enjoy each other. Let's go sit in the Jacuzzi under the stars." Chanel was a hopeless romantic. Donnell smiled. He took his shoes and socks off and let his jeans drop to the floor and stepped out of them along with his boxer briefs at the same time. Then Chanel pulled his shirt off and ran her hands down his pecs and abs and admired his chiseled body.

He lifted her blouse over her head and gently caressed her ample breasts in his hands. Then he kissed them. "Gotta taste my hersheys kisses. Gotta have my chocolate."
He unbuttoned her skirt and let it drop to the floor and she kicked her sandals off. Before they had reached the patio, Donnell had freed Chanel of her bra.

Chanel slid the screen door open and turned on the jets to the Jacuzzi as they both got in. It was just cozy enough for the two of them to have a romantic night. They sat in silence in each other's arms for a while. Then Chanel started running her mouth about things that weren't really all that important. Donnell wanted to shut her up. While Chanel was talking, Donnell's fingertips found their way to her nipples. He cupped one of her breasts with his left hand and she opened her legs, took his right hand, and guided it toward her vagina. He rubbed her clitoris again and she moaned as the combination of warm water and his fingers massaged her. He inserted his middle finger inside her and moved it in and out until she couldn't stand it anymore.

She turned and faced him and they kissed deeply under the moonlight. He then picked her up and she wrapped her legs around his back as he inserted his manhood inside her. She moaned as she felt him grow inside her.

"Ooh, Chanel! Girl!"

They continued to move in unison rhythmically until Chanel couldn't hold back any longer. She came with such a force that her whole body shook. A few seconds later, Donnell followed suit. The combination of the muggy night air and the steam from the Jacuzzi had made Chanel's hair fall.

They decided to retire to the bedroom. Chanel turned her stereo on low and put in a Sade CD. "...you're rulin' the way that I move, and I breathe your air, you only can rescue me, this is my prayer."

"I'm thirsty. Do you want anything?" Chanel asked Donnell.

"Yes, whatever you got is fine."

"Okay"

Donnell watched Chanel's round voluptuous ass jiggle as she walked away. *Damn, she's fine*, he thought to himself.

When Chanel came back from the kitchen with the drinks, *Cherish the Day* was still playing but Donnell was dozing off. She could see his eyes getting heavy.

"Wake up, sleepy head!"

He jerked wide awake and sat up. "Girl, make some noise next time! You scared the shit out of me."

Chanel smiled. "Here's your drink." Donnell guzzled down a Pepsi without taking a breath. Chanel demurely sipped hers. They each sat their glasses on the nightstand and Donnell dimmed the lights. They lounged in each others arms and fell asleep to Sade on repeat.

Chapter 2

Janai came staggering in the house filthy drunk. Jordan was on the couch watching game four of the finals between the Lakers and the Kings.

"Hell yeah!" Jordan jumped up off the couch when he saw Robert Horry make the shot of the century. "Whew! That's what I'm talkin' 'bout!" Horry saved the game in one second. Final score, one hundred to ninety nine...Lakers!

Jordan had been so caught up in the excitement of the game that he hadn't heard Janai enter. He just heard the water running in the bathroom. He went to check out what was going on and saw Janai doubled over the sink.

"I told you about drinking like that. It makes no sense for a woman to drink herself into oblivion. But you just continue to fill your body with that poison."

"Jordan, please just leave me alone right now," Janai said in between dry heaving.

Jordan just shook his head and walked back into the living room of their small apartment. He turned the volume up on the television and the commentators were still doing the post game interview with Robert Horry.

Janai was finally able to move again. She drenched a washcloth with cold water, wrung it out and then flopped down on the toilet seat. She tilted her head back to let the washcloth cool her face off in hopes that she could get rid of the drunken stupor. After about ten minutes she was able to make her way back to the bedroom to lie down.

Jordan decided to fix Janai a cup of coffee, despite the fact that he was disgusted with her for the umpteenth time. The two had numerous conversations about her drinking "habits". He crept into the room so as to not disturb Janai's hangover.
"Here Janai, this should make you feel a little better," he said standing over her.

Janai had her eyes closed but she wasn't asleep. She opened them slowly and tried to sit up to take the cup of coffee. She nearly lost her balance trying to sit up and suddenly grabbed her head and cringed.
"Oh God, I feel like a horse on a carousel ride. The whole room is spinning," she said.

Jordan helped her sit up so she could drink some of the coffee he had made for her. She was able to hold the cup and took a few sips of the coffee.

"You feeling a little better?" Jordan asked her.

"What the hell kind of stupid question is that? Do I look like I'm feeling any better?" Janai screamed at Jordan.

"You know what, Janai, you need to watch your mouth or..."

"Or what?!" Janai yelled, interrupting Jordan midstream. "Huh J, what the fuck you gon' do?" She tried to jump in his face but staggered and fell to her knees.

"Such a lady, come and talk to me when you're sober," he said in a disgusted tone. Jordan shook his head, grabbed a pillow and walked out of the bedroom. "I'll be on the couch." He slammed the door behind him, which caused Janai's head to howl in pain.

The next day, Janai woke up to the smell of breakfast. She heaved herself off the floor, where she had blacked out the night before. The sudden rise made her dizzy. Her head felt as if a sledgehammer had hit it. She managed to make her way to the nightstand by the bed and took two ibuprofens and drank the rest of the cold coffee Jordan had made for her.

Janai walked slowly toward the kitchen with her head down to see what Jordan had cooked for breakfast. She was famished. She was surprised to see a note from Jordan taped to the microwave.

Janai your breakfast is in the microwave. I really need some air so I'm leaving for a few hours. I hope you feel better. I love you, J.

She felt like such a heel after reading the note. She wanted to apologize to Jordan. Janai heard the ignition on Jordan's truck. Let me run and catch him before he goes, she thought to herself. She ran to the door, but lost her balance once again in the process. *Damn, I missed him!* She thought. She heated up her breakfast in the microwave. Jordan had really outdone himself. He left Janai pancakes, bacon and eggs.

Janai sat down in front of the TV and took pleasure in her meal. One of those infomercials promising instant results for a flat stomach was playing. She walked about three feet of over toward the patio door and opened it for some fresh air, but decided to keep the blinds closed. The brightness from the sunshine had started to make her head hurt.
"Umm," she moaned aloud. "This is so good." She sampled a little of her eggs and added a touch of pepper.
The infomercial was still running and she quickly grabbed a pen off of the table and a piece of newspaper that was lying to the left of her on the sofa. She wrote the number down and looked at her waist and grabbed a few rolls around her stomach and back area. She figured she'd just get Jordan to pay for it like he does everything else.

Once she got the number she flipped through the channels and settled on a movie that seemed interesting. It was one of those movies for women on *Lifetime*. She was halfway finished with her food when the phone rang. She looked at the caller ID on the cordless phone and immediately became angered when she noticed it was one of her boy toys she was seeing on the side.

"Robert, what the fuck is your problem?" she yelled into the phone. All the while her head was still pounding.

"Calm down, baby."

"Calm down hell. You are buggin'! How in the hell did you get my mothafuckin' number?"

"Don't worry about all that," Robert told her. "I was just trying to see you tonight, that's all. I haven't heard from you in a couple of weeks and I wanted to see if everything was alright."

"Look nigga, let me tell you something. First of all you're real sloppy. You know I live with my man. That's why I gave you my cell phone number. Second of all, you shouldn't even be tryin' to play games with me bro' because you have a whole lot more to lose that I do. I'm not the one that's married with four kids. So keep thinkin' it's a game and I will destroy that happy little home you got over there, a-ight," she retorted with much attitude.

"Okay, damn Janai, I'm sorry. Look let me make it up to you tonight. Sonya and the kids are driving up to Tennessee to see her mother. They'll be there until Monday. Why don't you let big daddy take care of you tonight?"

"I gotta see first," Janai replied. "I'll get up with you later," she told Robert as she slammed the phone down. She immediately pressed *60 on the phone pad to block his number. *That's a dumb ass nigga*, she thought as she finished eating the rest of her breakfast and watched the movie. Janai actually liked keeping him around because he bought her little trinkets, like expensive jewelry and clothes, and she liked that he took her out to places.

She got up and took her plate over to the sink to rinse it off and put it in the dishwasher. She went to her bedroom and decided to shower. As she reached for her bathrobe on the back of the door she caught a glimpse of her body in the mirror. Overall she was satisfied with her body; she just wanted to get rid of those love handles. But she was a very pretty woman. She was what a lot of people considered to be a "red bone."

She noticed that her short hairstyle was a mess and was starting to grow uneven, so she gave her stylist a call. She was lucky to get squeezed in on such short notice especially on a Saturday. Janai went to brush her teeth and take a shower. After she got all fresh and clean, she went to check the caller ID. She was disappointed. There was no call from Jordan.

After an hour passed, Janai called Jordan's cell. She figured she had allowed enough time to pass for him to cool off. She dialed the number and it went straight to voicemail. "Damn, his phone is off," she said aloud. She decided to call Chanel. "Whaddup, cow?" Janai howled to Chanel.

"Hey, what's up girl?"

"Just chillin' for a minute. I may hook up with Robert tonight, though. But first let me tell you what this dumb ass nigga did earlier today."

She rambled on about how he called her at home and how she gave him a piece of her mind.

"What?" Chanel inquired.

"Girl yeah, but I had a few choice words for him and I basically told him if he keeps playin' games with me, he'll regret it because he's the one with everything to lose…not me."

"That's crazy, Janai. But you're even crazier. You just better be careful, that's all I have to say about that. Because I do believe what goes around, comes around. And one day one of these women is going to fuck you up, girl. You better watch ya back."

"Yes, Reverend Jackson," Janai said sarcastically. "Anyway let me call you back later, I need to finish getting ready, I gotta go get my hair done."

Janai hurried down the hall to her bedroom and she put on a pair of white Capri pants and a turquoise halter top with a pair of flat turquoise sandals. She checked herself in the mirror and decided she needed some lipstick. She smoothed on her coral lipstick that complimented her light complexion. She grabbed her Coach bag and the keys to her old hooptie and bounced. On her way to the salon she called Robert and told him that she would take him up on his offer. She said she would call him when she was ready to meet him. She also instructed him to meet her at *Ruth Chris'* steak house. She loved being the boss. She loved the power she had over men. She could practically get anything she wanted.

Chapter 3

Donnell opened the door to his downtown loft and immediately noticed that his answering machine was flashing, indicating that he had messages. He pressed play. *"Hey Donnell, this is Tracey, I met you last week at the jazz club. I was trying to get together tonight if you have some time...give me a call...you have my number."* **BEEP!** *"Hey babe it's me, you never told me if you wanted to go to that new salsa club downtown. Call me back when you get this message. I love you."* **BEEP!**

His mind immediately began to race. He was pondering up what lies he would feed to Chanel. Hey always did....why stop now. He knew she'd believe whatever he told her. He picked up the cordless phone and walked over to the window where he could view the Atlanta skyline. He pressed number two on his speed dial and called Chanel. He fed her some bullshit about meeting with a potential client and then retiring to bed early. He said he had to meet with a client in the morning as well. Chanel didn't suspect a thing.

Donnell ran upstairs to get his cell phone. He had locked Tracey's number in his phone. He dialed her number.
"Hello?" she said in a high-pitched voice.
"Hello. Tracey?"
"Yeah."

"Hi, this is Donnell. I got your message and I was thinking maybe we can hook up tonight if you're still game."

"Yeah, it's cool with me," she said.

"You hungry?"

"Yeah," she said excitedly.

"So am I. Why don't I pick you up and we can go get something to eat at *201 Courtland.*"

"Ooh, yeah that sounds real nice."

Donnell shook his head as he hung up. He could tell by the tone of Tracey's voice that she wasn't used to being taken out or any of the finer things in life. He knew she'd be easy.

He looked in his closet to see what he'd wear for the evening. He decided on something casual. He chose his white linen outfit and a pair of crème canvas sandals. Donnell put on his doo-rag, showered and splashed on his favorite cologne. He put on some R. Kelly to help him get ready for the night. Thirty minutes had passed by and he had finished getting ready. He took his doo-rag off and brushed his fade in the back and sides of his hair and smoothed his waves in the crown of his head. He grabbed a stick of gum and headed for his SUV.

Tracey lived in Decatur, so Donnell hit I-20 eastbound. When he went to pick her up he didn't quite get what he expected.

Her mother came to the door in a bathrobe and some rollers. She hollered upstairs for Tracey to come down. Instead of Tracy coming downstairs, her two children decided to come down and interrogate Donnell. The door was cracked and since he had not been invited to come inside, he waited on the porch. The kids asked him where he was taking their mother and if he was going to be her new boyfriend. Finally, Tracy came down hoochiefied! She had blond weave and green contacts. She had on a short black mini skirt and a black bustier top and some high-heeled sandals. She also had two little butterfly tattoos that could be seen on her cleavage.

He took one look at her and thought to himself, *this chicken head ain't going nowhere with me looking like that.*
"Hey Donnell," she said in her high-pitched voice.
"Hi Tracey," he said dryly trying to sound interested.
"Just a minute, I forgot to get my purse." Tracey ran back upstairs. Donnell decided he would try to flake out on her. Just as he was opening the door on his side of the Navigator, Tracey had started walking towards him.
"Ok, I'm ready now," she said.

Tracey's whole family was watching from the window.
"So," Donnell said, "this is sort of a different look for you, huh?"

27

"Naw not really, I just had on a wig when you saw me the first time and I didn't have any contacts in that night. You got some gum?"

"Yeah, look in the glove compartment."

She took a piece of gum out and popped it and blew bubbles.

"This a real nice car you got here," she said as she smiled and looked at Donnell.

"Thanks." By this time, he was already irritated with her. Tracey had on tons of makeup but decided she needed some more powder and lipstick. Donnell looked at her and shook his head then looked out the driver's side window.

They finally made it to the restaurant. Donnell decided he would make the best of the situation. He got out and opened her door for her and set the alarm.

Everyone in the restaurant could tell they were like night and day. They all stared at her, and then glanced at him. Everyone was dressed to the nines.

Tracey noticed the aquarium behind the bar. "Ooh, this is real pretty, real pretty," she said loudly. "What kind of fishes are those?"

Donnell was embarrassed and kind of held his head down. A hostess greeted them and Donnell asked for something near the back of the restaurant. The atmosphere was nice and the lights were dim and a local jazz artist was performing.

"I don't like this song. I wanna make a request," Tracey said.

"Tracey you can't make a request. There's no deejay. It's a live performance." *Damn she has no scruples,* he thought. "Besides, I thought that you liked jazz since I did meet you at a *jazz* club."

"Naw, not really. See my cousin had told me that it was a nice place to meet nice men like yourself."

"I see." By this time Donnell just wanted to order, eat and hurry up to take this chicken head back where he found her.

They looked at the menu and Donnell decided on the lamb.

"I aint never had nothin' like this," Tracey exclaimed. "I thought this was a black restaurant, aint they got no chitlins' or nothin'?"

"No!" Now Donnell was extremely pissed.

"Well then I'll just have the chicken."

Shortly the waiter came back with their entrees. Donnell was so disgusted with her that he rushed through his dinner at a pace that would cause indigestion. Tracey also inhaled her food.

The waiter promptly brought the check to the table. Donnell laid his credit card on the tray and waited to sign the receipt. *Finally!* He thought to himself.

"Are you ready?" he asked Tracey. She nodded and grabbed her purse. As the two were leaving, Donnell was greeted by a familiar face.

Janai looked in her closet for something to wear for the night. Since it was breezy and warm, Janai chose her black cat suit; it *really* accentuated her large breasts and it made it appear as though she had some booty to show off as well.

She checked her appearance in the mirror and shook her hair to make it look fuller. Then she put on her gold hoop earrings and her black, strapless sandals. She grabbed some perfume and dabbed a little behind her ears and put some on the nape of her neck.

She looked at the clock on the wall. It showed 6:30p.m. She put on some of her favorite coral colored lipstick in a hurry and was intending on being at the restaurant by seven o'clock. Jordan reappeared just as Janai opened the door.

"I see you've decided to come home huh?"

Damn, he thought, *I hope she doesn't start any shit.* "Hey Janai."

"Hey Janai, nothin'! Nigga, where the hell have you been all day?"

Jordan really didn't enjoy confrontation at all, especially from Janai. She always seemed to make mountains out of molehills. And this time she really pushed the wrong damn buttons.

"The last time I checked, my mother lived in Seattle, Janai."

She was shocked he would even speak to her in that tone. The truth was he did work out and play ball with the fellas. Afterwards, he wasn't ready to come home so he took in a movie and then went for a bite to eat. He wasn't in a hurry to get back home to a drama queen.

Jordan threw his hands up and tried to walk away from Janai toward the bedroom.

She jumped in front of him and put her fingers in his face ranting and raving. She accused him of sleeping around. Jordan in turn said that she must be the one cheating since she always accuses him of it. He walked past her toward the bedroom.

"Don't walk away from me when I'm talkin' to you," she hollered as she grabbed his arm. Jordan jerked his arm from her grip and made her fall backwards. This of course, infuriated Janai.

"Oh, you gon' push me now!" She ran to the phone and dialed 911. She made a false domestic abuse report to the dispatcher. The operator told her the police would be there shortly.

"I got your ass now nigga."

Jordan looked like he wanted to choke Janai. He was livid! He had never been in trouble with the law and now it looked as if he was going to be spending the night in jail. He began to yell at her and just as he was walking up to her the police arrived.

Janai was nervous. She had never seen this side of Jordan. He had never put his hands on her or even so much as raised his voice. Janai was frightened and couldn't get to the door quick enough. After seeing the look in Jordan's eyes she told the police that it was all a big mistake. A misunderstanding.

The police looked at her suspiciously. "Ok, we won't make a report but if we have to come back out here tonight somebody's going to jail, you got it?"

"Yes," she told them. As soon as they left she looked at Jordan and he shook his head at her.

He thought she had truly lost all her marbles and he didn't know why he put up with her. She ran up to him and tried to hug and kiss him. "Jordan, I'm sorry."

"Janai, you say this all the time. And you know it won't be your last time pulling a stunt like this. Anyway look I'm exhausted. Let's just talk later when you get back. Besides, you look like you're going to the club anyway."

Remembering that she was late, Janai nodded in agreement.

She called Robert to tell him that she was on the way. He explained that there had been a mix up with the reservations and he wanted her to meet him at *201 Courtland*.

Robert was just getting out of his car when Janai pulled into the parking lot. As she was getting out of her car Robert walked up behind her and smacked her on the ass.

"I can't resist you, sweet thang. You look beautiful."

"Thanks," she said dryly. After all, he wasn't telling her anything she didn't already know.

They headed inside the restaurant. As Robert was opening the door for Janai she saw Donnell and his date walking out together.

"Well, well, well. What have we here?" Janai questioned in a haughty way while looking Tracey up and down.

"Hey Janai, what's up?" Donnell asked semi-nervously. He tried to pretend like everything was on the up and up.

"Oh I'm cool, but what's up with lil' Kim on crack?"

"Ooh, no you didn't. Honey I will take that as a compliment, 'cause I look damn good," she said while moving closer to Janai and swinging her hands in the air. "Donnell who is she anyway," Tracey beckoned.

"She's a friend of a friend."

"Tell her the rest, Donnell. Tell her I'm the friend of the woman you have been seeing for five years."

Robert tried to pull her arm. "Come on, Janai let's leave these nice people alone."

"Mind ya business, Robert." Chanel was her best friend and she wasn't leaving until she got the goods on Donnell.

"I think you need to take your friend's advice Janai," Donnell told her.

"No, go on and tell her about Chanel."

"Who's Chanel?"

"Oh, that's his girlfriend, sweetheart."

Donnell was livid. "Janai, you need to get you some business of your own, so you can stay out of mine. Come on, Tracey."

This was the time Janai wished she had a camera phone. But she reached in her purse just the same. She was about to give Chanel an ear full. Much to her chagrin her phone was dead. It needed to be charged. *Damn it!* She thought. She would just call her friend when she got home.

Several hours later they had eaten their meal and decided to go back to Robert's place for dessert. They drove to a beautiful subdivision in Stone Mountain. Robert opened the garage door with his remote and pulled in. Janai decided to park along side the curb.

When he got out of his car he motioned for her to drive in and park next to his car. He didn't want the neighbors to see him and tell his wife that he had a little visitor for the weekend.

They entered the oversized house from the side door through the garage. Janai plopped on the sofa and turned on the television.

Robert went upstairs and showered returning fifteen minutes later with nothing on but a towel. He walked in front of the TV and blocked Janai's view.

"Girl, I'm about to make you holler."

"Don't flatter yourself, Robert. But anyway before we do what you think we're about to do, you need to be giving me some cash."

"It's on my nightstand."

"Well it needs to be in my purse instead of on your nightstand."

"Ok, I'll be right back." He scurried his big body upstairs and was back down in a flash. "How's a couple o' hundred sound?"

"That'll work for right now."

"Now enough about money, let's talk about some honey," Robert stated as he eased over to her.

Janai had grown tired of sexing Robert, but continued to see him since he was good at giving up the cash.

He grabbed her butt and pulled her to him and started kissing her neck. She rolled her eyes and faked the funk. He unzipped the back of her cat suit so she could step out of it. He had undressed her to her thong and bra. He laid her on the couch slid her panties down, unsnapped her bra and tried to insert his penis.

"Wait a minute," she said. She didn't want him to drip sweat on her, so she decided to ride him. She mounted him and three minutes later it was all over. She quickly got up and went to the bathroom down the hall and showered.

When Janai came back into the living room, Robert was on the sofa fast asleep.

Janai left him that way. She got what she had come for.

Chapter 4

Donnell didn't appreciate Janai interrogating him. He thought about the whole situation as he drove from the restaurant back to his loft. He had decided that even though the chicken head got on his last nerve, he would get something out of the deal. After all, he did pay for dinner. *And pussy is pussy, so what the hell,* he thought.

During the drive back to his place, Donnell discovered that Tracey had the gift of gab. She just wouldn't shut up. She talked about everything under the sun. After about forty minutes, she finally decided it was time for him to do some talking.

"So you got a girlfriend, huh?"

"Fine time to ask don't you think?" Donnell said as he continued to watch the road.

"Well that's cool anyway 'cause my baby daddy is locked up, but he gettin' out in six months." Donnell simply shook his head.

Shortly they were at his place. As soon as Donnell opened the door it was like she had entered a palace. She noticed his beautifully waxed hardwood floor, the spiral staircase and the incredible amount of space this man had in his place.

Everything was very simplistic and elegant. Donnell had white, Italian imported leather in the living room and one picture of his parents on the wall. He loved his family, but he was extremely close to his Pops.

Donnell turned on some music and went into the kitchen and poured two goblets full of wine. He wanted her to be real loose. He handed her the glass of wine and she gulped most of it down. Then she got up and started to groove to the music. She eased over to Donnell and grabbed his crotch. He was already hard. He just stared at her with a grimace on his face and let her do her thing.

She unzipped his pants and pulled his underwear down to his ankles. Then, she began stroking Donnell's love stick up and down.

"I just wanna let you know I've never done anything like this before. I mean I don't have sex on the first date, and I just don't want you to think I do this to every man I meet," Tracey said in a seductively innocent voice. Just as Tracey began to pleasure Donnell with her expert tongue, his phone rang.

Damn! He figured it was Chanel. But at the moment he didn't feel the least bit guilty. All he knew was that he was about the bust a grape. He was getting the knob slobbed. He pushed Tracey's head back down so she could finish.

Tracey engulfed all of him into her mouth. As she stroked and sucked, Donnell felt like he was in heaven. He was moving in and out of her mouth relaxing with his hands behind his head. *First time my ass! She can suck a golf ball through a straw.*

Donnell finally came out of his clothes. He reached for a condom.

"Let's go upstairs," he told her. He didn't want to mess up his precious furniture. They both skipped up the spiral staircase to his Japanese inspired bedroom. There were black and red boxes with gold tassels everywhere.

Tracy pushed Donnell on the bed. "Here let me." She took the condom out of the gold wrapper and put it on with her tongue and mouth.

"Girl, you got talent."

She giggled. Donnell got up and turned her around and lifted her skirt up only to discover she didn't have on any panties. This excited him and he decided to hit it from the back. Fifteen minutes later they were done. Donnell laid on his back out of breath, and Tracey was, too.

A short while later Donnell slipped on a t-shirt and a pair of shorts to take her back home. He wouldn't dare allow her to stay the night.

Chapter 5

It was ten-thirty when Chanel awoke. Her nap lasted longer than she intended. She went to the kitchen to find something to eat. She found a leftover pork chop in the fridge and zapped it in the microwave.

Chanel went into the living room to watch a little television. She flipped channels and finally decided upon re-runs of Sanford and Son. It was the episode where Lamont wanted to be a Muslim and had changed his name. Thirty minutes went by and her phone rang. Since it was so late she wondered if it was Donnell. She was disappointed when she looked at the caller ID and saw that Janai was calling.

"What's up?"

"Your so called man, that's what," Janai told her matter of factly.

"What's that supposed to mean?"

Janai proceeded to dish all the dirt and gave her the run down.

"Are you serious?"

"Girl, yeah. I was trying to get in his business, but he just walked off. He was with some bitch named Tracey. I don't know where he got this skeeze. I mean the bitch had blonde weave all down her back and tattoos everywhere and shit."

"That lying mothafucka! He told me he had some business with a client and that's why we couldn't go salsa."

Janai was hyper. She reminded Chanel that they were best friends and that she was down for whatever. So if she wanted to go Left eye on his ass, that's what was up. But Chanel wasn't with the drama. She told Janai she was going to call him. Janai on the other hand tried to convince Chanel that she should pop up at his place. Donnell didn't like that and Chanel knew it. She also knew that anytime a nigga wants you to call first before you come over; it means he's trying to hide something or someone.

"Chanel, just handle your business and call me tomorrow. I'm going to bed."

Chanel sat a moment before she dialed his number and thought about how she would interrogate him. And then she thought about what his responses may be and how he might try to worm his way out of the questions.

She finally dialed the number. It rang three times and his voicemail picked up. She hung up and decided not to leave a message.

Janai's idea was becoming more and more attractive to her. She called Donnell again, this time trying his cell. It went straight to voicemail. Once again, she didn't leave a message.

The only time his phone is off is when he is at home, she thought. *Maybe I should go and see what's up. No, that would just make me look jealous and crazy. Besides, it's late.*

Chanel really *didn't* want to know. Besides, what was she going to do if it were true? Was she ready to stop seeing him altogether? *No one wants to be alone, and at least half a man is better than no man at all,* she thought. She decided to wait until the morning to call him and find out what was going on. She watched TV for an hour before falling into a restless sleep.

Donnell woke up at about nine o'clock the next morning. He thought about the night before and recalled how Tracey had gone down on him. Still, he decided to toss her number. He figured if she was that easy with him, she's probably easy with anyone and that's not a person he could respect.

His thoughts turned to Chanel. *What would he say to her about not answering his phone? She didn't leave a message, though. I wonder if that means Janai already told her what was up. Hmm?*

Donnell called Chanel. He figured if he beat her to the punch it would make it seem like he's not trying to hide or run from her. He was quickly trying to get his lies together before he called her in anticipation of what she might say or ask.

Chanel picked up with a sleepy voice sounding groggy.

"Hey baby, you still sleep?"

Her response was delayed. Her brain was a little hazy. "Yeah, I decided to sleep late."

"Well go on back to sleep and I'll call you back later."

"No, it's ok. I need to talk to you anyway."

Oh shit! She knows. "What about?"

"Didn't you hear the phone ring last night?"

"No, I was knocked out. I didn't hear a thing."

Chanel sat up in the bed. She needed to be one hundred percent alert for the rest of this conversation.

"Uh-huh, well let me just cut to the chase. Who the fuck is Tracey?"

"Tracey who?"

"Donnell, don't play with me. Janai told me you were out last night with someone named Tracey."

"Oh her. That's just one of my clients."

"But I thought you were supposed to be at home for the night. You lied to me, Donnell."

"No, I didn't lie. I was home and then she mentioned she was hungry and I hadn't eaten so I just thought we could have dinner together that's all. Just a meal to discuss business. No more, no less."

"Well the way Janai described her, she sure didn't sound like a client to me."

"Well she was. And what's with the third degree? Who you gonna believe? Me or that nosey ass friend of yours? She needs to mind her own fuckin' business. Now either you trust me or you don't. Now let's squash all this shit and go get some breakfast or something."

She knew he was only trying to change the subject. And although she wanted to believe him; she felt in her heart that he was lying. Her mother told her to always go with your first instincts; women's intuition. But she ignored it.

"Ok where?"

He smiled. *Whew, I dodged another bullet*! "How about that little hole in the wall, around the corner where they serve those peach pancakes?"

"Alright I'll meet you there in an hour."

Donnell knew he'd get his way. He had Chanel eating out of the palms of his hands.

Janai decided to get up early to grade papers. When she finished, she went into the living room and sat on the couch next to Jordan, who was watching sports center.

"Hey," she uttered in a low voice. She knew he wasn't really feeling her right about now.

"Good morning." He never took his eyes off of the television when he spoke to her.

"You still mad?"

"Why would I be mad, Janai?"

"Probably because I acted like an ass yesterday and the day before that."

"And the day before that," Jordan prompted. "You gotta cut that jealous shit out and if you're going to drink; learn how to handle your liquor."

"I know baby. I'm working on it." She was just glad he was speaking to her. "I'm sorry."

Jordan found it hard to stay mad at her for too long. Even through all the bullshit she took him through, he adored her and thought she was so beautiful. He pulled her closer to him and kissed her forehead and stroked her hair.

Shortly, Janai decided she was hungry and headed for the kitchen. Jordan noticed how sexy she looked in her tank top and panties. He gently grabbed her arm and pulled her down and started kissing her on the neck. That was her spot and he knew it. Janai found herself getting very wet. The ringing of the phone interrupted their groove. Jordan motioned for Janai to go and answer it.

"Uh-uh, let it ring." Janai pulled his chocolate bald head to her breasts as she leaned back against the arm of the couch. He pulled her tank top off and continued to kiss and lick her nipples.

They were both moaning and panting with excitement. She reached to feel his crotch. He was rock hard. She pulled his shorts down as far as she could, and he stood up to finish taking them all the way off. Janai sat up and kissed the head of his dick.

"Wait, I have a better idea." Jordan pulled her up and then laid on the couch. "Take 'em off," he motioned to her panties. She smiled and obliged him. He motioned for her to turn her body on top of his. He scooted down so that they could give each other 69 ways to make each other holler. Then Janai

44

rode Jordan 'til the cows came home. They did their thing until they both exploded. Janai had little beads of perspiration on her forehead and nose. Jordan was out of breath. They both just laid there for a second.

"Come on, let's shower together," Janai suggested. Jordan followed behind so he could watch her walk. Janai turned the water on and checked the temperature to ensure it was just right. Not too hot, not too cold. She got in and let the water trickle down her face. Jordan got in behind her. As soon as she bent over and picked up the soap, it was all over. They went at it again. They were in the shower until it ran cold.

Just as Chanel was about to head out to meet with Donnell for breakfast, her phone rang. It was her cousin Micki.

Micki and Chanel were more like best friends than cousins. When they were both back in L.A. they did everything together. But after graduating from high school, Micki moved to Chicago to attend college. She was older than Chanel by two years.

The two had spoken days earlier and Micki was calling to let Chanel know that she had enough of the windy city and their 'below zero' temperatures. She had an interview scheduled with *B of A* in Atlanta. And although she didn't need the job, she enjoyed working. Micki was mature and way ahead of her time. She learned how to invest at a young age and she had been sitting on a fortune for some time now. She was simply calling to let Chanel know what day and time her flight would arrive. Chanel offered for her cousin to stay with her for as long as she needed. After the two hung up, Chanel did what she does best, run to Donnell.

After they had breakfast, they spent the whole day together. Donnell took her shopping. And even though it seemed as if Chanel believed him, guilt got the best of him. He bought her a Nefertiti necklace and had it inscribed for her. It read, for my *Nubian Queen*. And no doubt it cost him a small fortune.

After their outing Donnell decided he would spend the night at Chanel's place. He wanted her to thank him properly. Hours later they were both fast asleep. Donnell had his arms around Chanel and they were cuddled up in the spoon position. Donnell was startled awake by his cell phone at two in the morning. He looked at the number on the phone and recognized his parents' number in L.A. It was his father. His voice was somber. He was calling to tell him that his mother had a massive heart attack.

"Wha...what happened?" Donnell asked sounding choked up. Chanel sat up and turned on the lamp.

Apparently her attack came out of the blue to both of them. She was just folding clothes, stood up and grabbed her chest and then collapsed. They immediately wheeled her into surgery.

Donnell lost it. He dropped the phone. His mother was his heart. Chanel picked up the phone and briefly spoke with Donnell's father. She had tears in her eyes as he spoke to her.

She sympathized with Donnell's father. "I'm so sorry Mr. Black. I know there isn't much I can do, but I'll pray."

"Thank you. Your kind words mean a lot dear."

Donnell sat up and was able to regain his composure long enough to speak with his father again. "I'm sorry Dad I never even asked you, how you were holding up?"

"I just feel helpless, son. But we just gotta keep praying. God's will is whatever He deems it."

Donnell told his father that he loved him and he would be there as soon as he could. He needed to contact the airlines.

The next morning, Chanel dropped Donnell off at the airport for an eight-thirty flight.

"Donnell call me if you need anything. Your mother is in my prayers."

Chanel knew that Donnell felt as bad as he looked. He hadn't been able to get back to sleep after talking with his father. He just nodded his head in agreement. He gave Chanel a quick peck on the lips and went to check in for his flight.

Chapter 6

Four and a half hours later Donnell arrived at LAX. He hadn't bothered to check his bag. He didn't want to prolong seeing his mother. He went out to the curbside near ground transportation and flagged down a taxi cab driver.

"Where to?" the cabbie asked him.

"Cintinella Hospital. And don't bother taking the scenic route, I'm in a hurry." He knew that the cab drivers would occasionally take the longer way as a means to keep the meter running longer.

Traffic was thick as usual so it took him forty-five minutes to get to the hospital. When he arrived, he went straight to the critical care unit and saw his father in the waiting area.

"Dad?" He immediately embraced and comforted his father. "How's Momma?"

"The same."

"Where is she? I want to see her."

"Down the hall, in room 205."

Donnell nodded and headed to room 205. His father wanted to give him some private time with his mother so he waited in the lobby.

Donnell paused before he entered the room. He was trying to be strong for his family. He also wanted to brace himself for what was behind the door.

"Oh, Momma!" he cried out with tears flushing his face. Donnell's mother had tubes running from both arms and her mouth. It pained Donnell to see his mother in this state.

He pulled up a chair near the bed and took his mother's hand in his. Then he gently stroked her beautiful, white, silky hair. She looked old to him, yet Annabelle Black was only sixty-five. In Donnell's mind, she still had a lot of living to do.

"Momma, wake up it's me...Donnell, your son. Can you hear me?" He felt so helpless. But he just began speaking from the heart.
"Momma, you can't leave us now. We need you. You've got so much life left in you. Don't give up, Momma. Just fight. Remember how you used to tell me that when I was younger? Just fight. Fight for whatever it is that you want. You always believed in me. You never gave up on me, Momma. Well guess what? I'm not giving up on you. I need you. Dad needs you too. We love you. Come back to us."

There was silence and Donnell found himself at a loss for words, so he prayed:
"Dear God, please don't take my mother from me right now. I know we all have to go sometime, but this isn't my mother's time. Not right now. I know I don't pray like I should, but if you've never heard me before, please hear me now. I don't know what I'd do without my mother. My family is all I have."

There was a knock at the door and the nurse had come to check his mother's vitals. Donnell's father walked in. "Nurse how's my wife?"

"Mr. Black, there's been no change, if we find out anything new, you'll be the first to know." She said this without feeling, as if she had become immune to these types of situations.

Annabelle struggled to open her eyes. She focused slowly on both of them. "Hey," she said with a raspy voice. "What are you two staring at?"

Both Donnell and his father heaved a sigh of relief. She's back and she still had her wits about her.

"Momma, you gave us quite a scare."

"I'm sorry, baby. How's my handsome son?"

"I'm worried about you."

"No need son, I'll always be alright as long as I have God. Now enough about this hospital talk. I want to talk about you and that pretty woman you got back in Atlanta."

Donnell had always enjoyed conversations with his mother. He tried the best he could to soak up the wisdom. His mother asked him about marriage and he brushed it off. The truth was he thought about it, but just like every other man, he felt as if he would be missing out on something if he got married. Plus, he didn't want to be tied down to one woman when there were a myriad to choose from. He enjoyed that player lifestyle. His mother sensed that he was apprehensive about marriage.

"Don't miss out on a good thing. Your daddy almost lost me because of his pussy-footing around."

"What? Dad was a player?"

"He tried to be, but I wouldn't let him. He went out there sniffin' around thinkin' there was something better than me. I told him, he could go out there if he wanted to, but don't come back. 'Cause Ms. Annabelle is gon' be gone."

Donnell was in stitches over his parents' stories. The nurse interrupted them again to give Mrs. Black her medication. Annabelle was coherent for about ten more minutes, then she drifted off to sleep. Donnell's father began nodding as well. Donnell insisted that his father get some rest. He knew he had been up all night and all morning. But his father refused to leave his wife's side. Donnell knew his father was adamant on staying with his mother. So, he arranged for one of the nurses to bring in a roll-away bed. Mr. Black fell asleep rather easily.

Donnell was exhausted. He had also been up for several hours and had not eaten. Donnell decided to go home to rest and freshen up. He wrote his father a note, just in case he should wake up while he was gone. Then he grabbed his father's keys.

Surprisingly there was no traffic. Donnell made it to his parents' home near Watts in less than twenty minutes. Their home was an older home with a screened in porch, crawl space and bars on every window and door.

Once inside Donnell began to feel nostalgic. He examined the rearranged living room with family portraits displayed. His graduation picture with him in his cap and gown was displayed, as well as his many accomplishments from Cal State-Berkeley.

He sat on the couch and picked up the photo album. He flipped though the pages and stopped when he saw his parent's wedding picture. He thought briefly about what his mother had said. *Me married?* He relished the thought of him and Chanel. Just as quickly as he thought about it, he quickly dismissed it. *Hell no!*

He thumbed through some more pictures and saw his best friend, Jeff. They had known each other since third grade. Later on they even went to the same college. Jeff was a constant reminder to him of how quickly your life could change in a matter of seconds.

They were at a barbeque in Inglewood one weekend and Donnell went to the bathroom. Less than three minutes later he heard five gun shots and people screaming. He laid low for a moment and then went to investigate when he thought it was safe. He went back outside and saw a crowd of people surrounding his best friend in a pool of blood.
Jeff was dead at the tender age of twenty-two, just two weeks before their college graduation.

Donnell slammed the photo album shut and jumped up off the couch and went to his old bedroom. He opened the door and the room had a stale smell to it, since it really didn't get used.

Donnell flopped down on the bed and decided to give Chanel a call. He updated her on his mother's condition. Chanel sent her love and prayers.

He leaned back on the bed with intentions of only doing some deep thinking. However, as he lay back, his eyes grew heavy and he was out for the next three hours. It was after five when he woke up. *I guess I needed that*, he said to himself.

Donnell showered and changed. Then he went to his parent's room to get a change of clothes for his father as well.

Before leaving the house he went to the kitchen to check the fridge. He was starving. He noticed there wasn't anything already made to be eaten. Everything had to be cooked. He decided on a burger and his dad loved chili from *Fatburger*.

Upon his arrival back to the hospital, he and his father chowed their food down in minutes. Mrs. Black was still out of it. But something started happening. One of the monitors gave off a loud, blood-chilling shrill. Both Donnell and his father looked over to see Annabelle thrashing around violently. Several doctors and nurses rushed in to push Donnell and his father out of the way. Donnell and his father demanded to know what was going on. They were told they would know her prognosis shortly. She was being rushed into surgery. They were both worried and although Donnell tried to convince his father that everything would be fine, he didn't sound too confident himself.

The two kneeled down and said a prayer for Annabelle Black.

Chapter 7

The school bell rang, indicating the end of yet another school day. Janai gathered her things as quickly as the children ran out of her classroom.

Mondays always gave her the blues, but for some reason she felt a little more down than usual. It was her Father's birthday, and also a few weeks before Father's day. She tried to make those thoughts vanish out of her head.

"All I need is a few drinks," she said out loud to herself.

She grabbed her purse, locked her classroom door and headed home. As soon as she made it through the front door she kicked her shoes off and flopped on the couch underneath the ceiling fan.

Twenty minutes later, Jordan walked in with one arm behind his back, flashing Janai his dazzling smile. He had a Fed-Ex delivery near their home and decided to drop in on her. He handed her a single red rose.

"This is for you," he said giving Janai a peck on the lips.

Her face immediately lit up. "You're so sweet. Thank you, Jordan."

He knew that he didn't have a lot of money to take her out but he improvised.

"I was thinking, after I finish my last delivery we can go to the park and have a nice little picnic." Jordan suggested.

Janai frowned at the idea. "It's too hot outside for a picnic, J. Let's just stay in and watch a movie or something tonight."

Jordan was a little deflated. "Alright, whatever you want to do."

Janai grinned at the thought of getting her own way.

■■

A few hours later when Jordan arrived back home; he saw Janai sprawled out on the couch watching TV with a bottle of wine on the coffee table. He shook his head. He also noticed that she hadn't even bothered to get a wine glass. She just took it straight from the bottle. She sat up on the couch when she heard Jordan come in. Somehow she thought she was gaining some composure. And Janai knew how Jordan felt about her drinking, but she did it anyway. Jordan took the bottle away from her. There was somewhat of a silent understanding. He hadn't said much, but she knew what was going on and what was up.

Once he showered and unwounded a bit he wanted to spend some quality time with Janai.

"Baby, I picked up some DVD's. You want to watch a movie now?"

Janai shrugged her shoulders. "I don't care. Whatever you want to do," she said quickly placing something underneath the couch cushion.

Although Janai had an attitude most of the time, this time seemed different to Jordan. She seemed distant to him.

"What's wrong?"

"Nothing."

"Look, I know you and I can tell that something is obviously bothering you. Now what's up?"

"Damn it! I said I was fine! Can't you understand English?"

Jordan walked closer to the couch and pulled out whatever it was Janai hid beneath the couch cushions. To Jordan's surprise, it was an old photograph of a man who looked just like Janai.

Janai didn't have the energy to argue. She had been in a depression.

Jordan showed Janai the picture in such a way as if she had never seen it before.

"It's your Dad, isn't it?"

Janai nodded. "Look I just want to forget about him today alright?"

"Why, what's today?"

"Look, it's my father's birthday alright. But it's not up for discussion J, I mean it" she said rolling her eyes.

"I didn't know, Janai. But, you don't have to feel like you have to keep secrets from me. I'm not going to hurt you. You know that. You can talk to me. Now what's up?" He moved in closer to her and rubbed her shoulders to help her get comfortable and to let her know everything was going to be fine.

"I was just hoping to forget the past." Janai hesitated for a moment, until she realized it might feel good to release what she had been holding back. And deep down inside she knew that Jordan wasn't the type of person to play on her vulnerabilities. So she continued to tell her story.

"The reason I never talk about my parents is because it brings up bad memories." The whole time she talked, she kept her head down. Janai didn't want to risk making eye contact with Jordan. He might be able to see right through her and play on her vulnerabilities and she couldn't have that.

Janai got up off the couch and walked over to the window. She decided if she didn't face Jordan she would not cry.

"Well..." Janai continued, "my father was an abusive alcoholic. He never hit me, but he used to beat my mother silly. Who, in turn took out her frustration on me. Eventually, my father left. This made my mother depressed and she would beat me even more." Janai turned to look at Jordan to see if he was still listening.

Jordan was staring intently at Janai with a saddened look on his face.

"Not only did she physically abuse me, but she also verbally abused me. She called me everything, but a child of God. I finally couldn't take it anymore and ran away when I was fifteen years old. I hate them both."

"What about staying with some other family members," Jordan interrupted.

"My father was an only child and I never really knew my aunts from my mother's side. And my grandmother died when I was ten. She was the only person who truly loved me." A single tear dropped from the corner of her eye.

Jordan tried to hug her and dry her tears. She turned away from him and sat back on the couch. "It's cool. I'm alright. You don't have to baby me, or feel sorry for me. I'm always gon' be alright as long as I got my juice," she said as she picked up the wine bottle.

"Janai, don't you get it? You're doing what your father did for years and all you're doing is covering it up, masking the pain. When you come down off that high, you're right back where you started, hurt, lonely and sad. You have to confront these feelings in order for them to go away."

"Look Mr. Psychologist, everyone can't have a perfect fuckin' family like you. You had a happy fuckin' childhood; you grow up, go to college, get married, have children and live happily ever after. I thought that shit was only in the story books, but I guess you're the exception."

She walked over to the patio door and stared out the window. "See that's why I like the bottle. 'Cause it don't have shit to say. It don't talk back. It just makes me feel good."

"Stop it! Stop trying to act so hard. You don't have to do that with me." Jordan walked over to her and touched her shoulder and turned her towards him.

By then, Janai's face was drenched. She sobbed uncontrollably, like she was a little child. This had been a long time coming. Jordan rocked Janai in his arms and told her that everything was going to be alright.

Chapter 8

Chanel had arrived home rather late. She had gone out for a drink after work. She had tried to get in touch with Donnell at his parents' place, but she wasn't able to reach anyone. He hadn't called her on her cell phone either. She checked the caller ID box in the bedroom and the voicemail to see if he had called. Nothing. No Donnell. She hoped that everything was okay. She also noticed that Janai hadn't called either. She had called her earlier and left a message.

She disrobed and decided to take a bubble bath. She pinned the back of her hair up and lit five scented candles consisting of a mixture of pineapples, peaches, pears, and papaya. She got in, closed her eyes and let the warm water take her to another galaxy.

The next morning she was awoken at five A.M by a telephone call. The call came through as a private number.

To Chanel's surprise, it was Donnell, and he sounded rather exhausted. Chanel could sense something was wrong.

Donnell broke the news to her. He had lost his mother. He explained to her that his mother had gone into convulsions again, and during the surgery her body just wasn't responding to the procedure or the medication.

This upset Chanel a great deal. Her eyes welled up in tears as Donnell was explaining what happened and how he was feeling. She remembered what it was like when her father had surgery and although he lived, everyone thought that he wouldn't make it. So she knew how Donnell was feeling, how hurt he was.

Chanel wanted to hop on the first plane to LA, but Donnell discouraged her. He didn't want to be around anyone. He told Chanel he needed some space and some time to think. Not to mention making funeral arrangements, especially after his father had become too upset to take care of all of that.
She was hurt that he didn't want her help, especially in a crisis such as this. Donnell told her he would call in a few days once he had a chance to assess everything and make funeral arrangements.

■■■

Several days had passed since Chanel had spoken with Donnell. She was on the way to the airport to pick up her cousin, Micki, from Chicago.
The flight was delayed by twenty minutes, but alas, Micki was here.

"Hey Hollywood!" They hugged. "Girl, you got it goin' on."

"So do you, little cuz." Micki's cinnamon skin was practically glowing. She stood two inches taller than Chanel. She sported a white pantsuit with a pink shirt with a wide collar underneath, and some pink strapless sandals and a pair of dark shades.

The whole ride home they giggled like two school girls and gossiped about other family members.
Once they arrived at Chanel's, she showed her around the place and Micki commented on how much she liked it and how great taste definitely runs in the family. Chanel and Micki both got their expensive tastes from their mother's side of the family.

After Chanel finished the tour of the place she showed Micki where her room was. Micki was tired and wanted to take a shower.

As Chanel walked back into the living room, she noticed the phone was flashing for her to check her voicemail. Donnell had called. She had only missed him by about fifteen minutes. He called to give her the information about the funeral. It would be held the following Saturday.

Chapter 9

Micki's interview was very successful. She got the job. She was offered a handsome salary with lots of fringe benefits. In addition, she received a huge corner office that overlooked downtown Atlanta.

Micki called Chanel with the news.

"I got the job!"

"See, I told you Micki."

"They want me to start in three weeks, so I don't have a lot of time to relocate. And I'll also need time to find a home. I'm not trying to crowd you."

"Please! I told you my home is your home. You're family, so don't even trip. You can stay with me, for as long as you need."

"I hear you talking, but I'm not going to wear out my welcome. Anyway, this calls for a celebration."

That night the girls went out to celebrate and enjoyed a night of black Chippendale dancers. Chanel had invited Janai, but she declined. She wanted the two cousins to have some time to themselves. Besides, Janai had other things on her mind.

■■

Jordan and Janai had just finished their dinner and were enjoying a few glasses of wine. And as usual, Janai picked one of her many fights with Jordan, yet again. She told him that she was tired of staying at home and wanted to go on a vacation cruise to the Caribbean. Although, it sounded real good to

Jordan, he told her that he was trying to save money. He had financial goals. After all, one of them had to have some discipline.

"Maybe next year Janai," he told her.
"Next year? Fuck that! I don't know why I'm with your broke ass anyway. You don't ever have any money!"
Janai continued to act like a spoiled little bitch. She got up off the couch and walked in the kitchen. She was so infuriated with the whole situation that she purposely knocked the vase and single rose off the counter top. She told Jordan that he was so cheap that he probably got the rose from the grocery store for a dollar.

Jordan couldn't believe how selfish and ungrateful she was being. Besides, he took good care of her. He paid the rent and utilities. He buys groceries. Hell, he even cooks! All Janai has to do is go to work and come home.
"You really need to grow up, Janai. I would think you of all people would appreciate a good man doing nice things for you….considering."
"What's that supposed to mean?"
Jordan realized he had struck a nerve. "Nothing. Never mind."
"No, you were referring to my father, weren't you?"
You son of a bitch!"
She picked up a glass off the counter top and threw it at him, but missed.

"How dare you throw something in my face that I shared with you?"

She was angry and on the verge of tears.

As angry as Jordan had become he didn't want to hit Janai, but he wanted to shake her. He knew it was only the liquor talking. He felt like if he had said anything else one of them would have gone to jail that night. So instead he decided to isolate himself in their bedroom.

Janai was beside herself. She was still ranting and raving in the living room when her cell phone rang. It was her sugar daddy, Robert. Janai went out on her apartment balcony to finish her conversation. She didn't want Jordan to overhear. Robert told her he was calling to see when she'd be free again. He wanted to take her shopping, but not for clothes. This time he wanted to take her car shopping. He told her that before they go shopping, she was to meet him at the Shiny Fox motel. Janai knew what time it was. She felt like it was okay to give up a little when she's getting a lot in return.

The next morning when Janai woke up she looked at the clock with blurred vision and suddenly realized she was late for work. She had drunk too much the night before. She didn't even remember putting herself to bed. In actuality, she passed out on the couch and Jordan put her in the bed. She quickly jumped out of bed and started to get ready. She pulled an outfit from her closet that didn't require any ironing. Janai called the school and let them know that she was running late.

She hoped the superintendent, Mrs. Dean, didn't get wind of this. Mrs. Dean was an old white woman, who was a stickler for the rules. She was strictly by the book.

Janai finished getting ready in record time. Once she started heading to work she decided to call Robert. She told him that she wanted to go to the dealership that afternoon rather than wait until the weekend. Robert was more than happy to oblige.

On her drive to work, Janai reflected on her recent exploits. She thought about how she treated Jordan all the time. She thought about Robert and his expensive gifts and money. She thought about future ventures that might potentially have her set financially.

"Shit, I gotta come up," she said aloud. "Humph! I just gotta do what I gotta do."

Chapter 10

Donell was still in shock over his mother's death. His father was in worse shape. He was withdrawn; refusing to talk, eat, or drink. He didn't even want to get out of bed.

Donnell was burning the candles at both ends. He was trying to look after his father and take care of himself. He didn't know whether he was coming or going. He found himself praying more than he ever had. He felt like he needed to relieve some stress. He needed to talk to someone. It was early morning in Los Angeles, but his body was still operating on Eastern Time zone. He picked up the phone and dialed Chanel's number.

"Hello?"

"Hey Chanel, how you doin', babe?"

"Donnell?" She was surprised. She hadn't expected to hear from him so soon. "I'm fine. The real question is, how are you?"

"Stressed. Angry. Sad."

"Those wounds will heal in time, Donnell."

"I know, but I'm just trying to get through today."

"You're up kind of early aren't you?"

"Yeah, it's early here, but my body hasn't really adjusted since I've been back. But I haven't really been sleeping anyway."

"How's your father?"

"I'm worried about him. He's withdrawn. He hardly gets out of bed, unless I force him to move around,

68

take a walk, or eat a little something. I don't know what to do. That's why I called; I just needed to vent a little."

"Well you know that you can call anytime." Chanel got a smile out of him.

"That's one thing I really love about you. You are always there for me."

"And I always will be." Chanel shared his brief joy.

"So, anyway what's on your agenda for today?" Donnell asked, trying to sound normal.

"Micki and I are going shopping and then later tonight we're going out."

"Has she met Janai yet?"

"No."

"Oh-oh."

"What?"

"Oh I don't have to say a word. You know your friend."

"There's nothing wrong with her. She just has issues like we all do."

"Yeah but her shit is a little more deeply rooted in that brain of hers." They both chuckled.

"Yeah, but it'll be alright."

"Well, I'm going to let you go now; I just needed to hear a friendly voice."

"Okay. Are you sure you don't need me to fly out there sooner?"

"No, I can hold everything down until you get here."

"Okay, I'll talk to you later."

After they hung up, Donnell felt alone. He was surprised by how much he missed Chanel.

At two o'clock in the afternoon Janai got a call from Robert. He told her he had a few loose ends to tie up on the home front and she was to meet him at the Shiny Fox motel. It was in a seedy part of town and Robert knew no one would catch him over there.

After the phone call, Janai went back to her bedroom to pick out a semi-sexy outfit. She wanted to set everything out just right, so she could get the car she wanted. She was thinking about maybe an Acura, BMW, or the new Benz.

She rummaged through her closet and found a beautiful, pink chiffon dress that she hadn't worn in a while. She slipped it on with ease. To her surprise, she had lost a little weight. She noticed it wasn't as tight around her waist as it had been in the past. She looked in the mirror and noticed her hair was out of place.
She grabbed her soft bristled brush and began stroking her hair. It had a lot of body so it bounced back in place. She put on a little eye shadow and mascara and her favorite lipstick. She dabbed a little perfume behind her ears and those private, hot spots.

She looked in the mirror and was satisfied with her appearance. She pursed her lips together to spread the lip color some more. Fussed with her hair one last time, and pushed her breasts up to reveal more cleavage.

When she got to the hotel she tried to check in under her name. She discovered that it had not yet been paid for which meant that Robert hadn't shown up yet. She took a seat in the lobby and decided to send him a text message. It read: ROBERT U NEED 2 HURRY UP! I'M AT THE SHINY FOX. THE ROOM IS UNDER MY NAME AND IT HASN'T BEEN PAID 4 YET…SO I'M WAITING ON U.

Less than five minutes had passed and Janai received a reply message on her phone. IT read: I'M ON MY WAY! I WILL B THERE SHORTLY! Ten minutes later, Robert walked in the hotel lobby. "That was quick," Janai said to him. "I left a little earlier than I expected, but I thought you were going to call me." Janai had a puzzled look on her face. "I sent you a text message." "Hmm. Well I didn't get a message or anything. Might've been poor reception in the area I was driving in. Anyway, you look gorgeous." Janai thought about the reply she received back to her phone. Then she figured if she sent it to the wrong number accidentally, someone could've just been playing on her phone.

Once they got to the room, Janai wanted to make sure she was going to get what she wanted. Robert told her she could pick out whatever she wanted. Of course since she was greedy she wanted to go for the gusto and get that new Benz. But Robert quickly reminded her Jordan may get suspicious, since a Mercedes is somewhat expensive on a teacher's salary. She agreed and then decided upon an Acura. In her mind she was being practical.

Janai got the formalities out of the way and handled her other business with Robert. They were done in less than thirty minutes. Janai showered and brushed her bob back in place. She was done quickly and told Robert she'd be in her car waiting on him. She was going to follow him to the dealership.

Walking to her car, Janai noticed a woman whose face looked familiar, but she just couldn't place it. Robert finally came out and they headed to the dealership. As Janai began to follow Robert she noticed the strange woman nearby in a red car, start her engine. She kept checking her rearview mirror and noticed the woman had begun to tail Janai. Robert signaled to get off on the next exit and so did Janai. She was still watching the person behind her. The little red car never got over. It kept going and zoomed down I-75.

"Whew! It's just my imagination," Janai thought out loud.

She and Robert had finally made it to the dealership. When Janai got out of the car and met Robert near the entrance she had a strange look on her face. She told Robert she thought a woman in a red car was following her and furthermore that she thought the woman resembled Sonya, Robert's wife.

Robert insisted that she was at the house when he left and that her car was green. And out of all the places in Atlanta, she would not have known to come to that particular hotel, not to mention it was in the hood.

An hour later, Janai drove off the lot in a brand new, fully loaded, silver Acura. She had convinced Robert to put it in her name and he would be making all the payments. She was ecstatic.

On her way home she thought, *now that's how you play them niggas. Just make sure you gettin' somethin' out the deal.*

When she got home she was glad that Jordan wasn't home at the moment. She couldn't wait to call Chanel to brag and boast.

"Chanel, not only did I get the car, but it is in my name and that nigga is makin' the payments. So now I'm through with Robert. I got what I wanted, some money and some expensive gifts. Now I can move on and conquer the rest of the world."

Shortly, after their conversation, Jordan arrived. She lied and told him that she traded her old car in and that she had been saving her funds. Jordan thought this was highly suspect, but he didn't say a word. He had never known Janai to save for anything. In fact, she was always crying broke and asking him for money.

That evening Chanel had finished getting herself ready to go out for a "Girls night out" with Micki. She decided to call Janai and kill some time while Micki finished getting ready.

As they were talking Janai was interrupted with another call of her own. It was Robert.

He was frantic. Apparently, the day he and Janai met at the hotel, he had inadvertently mixed up their cell phones. So when Janai thought she was sending a text to Robert it was really his wife Sonya who responded to it. He said she was now interrogating him about her name and where Janai lived.

"Yo, you actin' all paranoid and shit. I know I'm not the first woman you've fucked around with since you've been married. Look, all you gotta do is tell her that you don't know where I live because we always met at a hotel or something. And as far as the name is concerned, just give her a fake name. Just do enough to satisfy her. Now handle your business, 'cause I gotta go." She hung up with him and clicked back over to Chanel.

Janai gave Chanel an earful of what happened and what Robert had told her. Even though she and Janai were friends that didn't necessarily mean that she agreed with how Janai carried herself as a woman. And of course she gave Janai the third degree. Chanel definitely wasn't a saint, but she had some morals about herself and would never get involved with another woman's man, especially a married man.

The rest of the week went quickly. Micki went back to Chicago to pack her things. Janai was home free. She had gotten the car she wanted plus a few nice gifts. And Chanel had flown to Los Angeles to attend the funeral for Donnell's mother.

Donnell decided that he would fly back to Atlanta with Chanel and occasionally check in with his father about once a week. His father had insisted that he wanted to stay where he could always remember his late wife. That had been their home for almost forty years.

A month later, Micki moved out of Chanel's condo and into her own home in the Cascades. She found her position at *B of A* fulfilling and wanted to have a barbeque instead of the traditional housewarming. Everyone was young and restless and would soon go through some *extreme circumstances*.

Chapter 11

The phone rang and Jordan answered it. It was a woman asking to speak to Janai.

"Sure. Just a minute. Janai? Phone."

She was just coming out of the bathroom and walked towards the kitchen.

"Hello? Helloooo?" Janai looked at Jordan in puzzlement. There was no one there and all she got was a dial tone.

"Who was it, Jordan?"

He shrugged his shoulders. "I didn't ask."

Janai checked the caller ID box to see who it was. It came up as a private number.

Janai was exhausted. She yawned as she walked toward the freezer.

"You alright? You look a little flushed, Janai?"

Her eyes shifted. "Yeah, I'm alright. Just a little tired that's all. Since I took on teaching summer school, I've been wiped out. I think I'll feel better if I eat some of this ice cream in here."

She reached into the freezer and got a pint of rocky road ice cream. Jordan continued to watch her as she walked from the kitchen to the couch. She had decided to watch television with him.

"What?" she said as she noticed Jordan staring at her.

He told her she looked like she was gaining weight. And surprisingly she didn't hit the roof. In fact, she agreed with him. She told him that it was probably all of the junk she had been eating lately and that she needed to start eating a little healthier as well as hit the gym.

Placing his hand on his heart he told her it didn't matter how big she got and he would love her no matter what. She would always be beautiful to him, because that's the type of man Jordan was.

This infuriated Janai and she just flipped out on him. "So you must think I'm gon' be a big ass fuckin' whale or something, huh? What you wanna call me now? Shamu?"

Jordan was stunned.

She didn't even give him time to respond or apologize if that's what he wanted to do.

"No, Janai, I was just…"

"Just what, J? You know what, J…fuck you!" She stormed off with her pint of ice cream and headed for the bedroom and slammed the door. Janai wolfed down her ice cream then and called Chanel.

Chanel knew her friend very well. As soon as she picked up the phone and heard the tone of Janai's voice she knew that something was wrong. And of course she prodded until she got a satisfactory answer out of her.

Janai quickly hopped off the bed and slowly opened the door to peep down the hall. She wanted to make sure Jordan was not on the phone. He was watching TV.

"I'm late Chanel."

"Late with what? Your rent? Girl, you need some money?"

Janai rolled her eyes. "No fool, I mean my period. I'm pregnant."

Chanel was only slightly surprised. She thought that Janai would be happy since she adored children. After all, she is a teacher. Ironically, though, she does love children, but doesn't want to have any of her own. She knew it was a big difference in spending a few hours with someone else's kids versus spending the next 18-20 years with your own.

"Chanel, I ain't trying to be nobody's mama."

"So what are you going to do?"

She told Chanel that she would probably terminate the pregnancy and she had no intentions of talking to Jordan about it. She felt like it was her body and he didn't have to carry it. Not to mention she knew he wouldn't go for an abortion…not the type of man he is. She also had another slight issue to deal with in all of this. She wasn't even sure if Jordan was the father.

"So you might be pregnant with a married man's baby? Damn, Janai didn't you use condoms?"

"No."

"I'm sorry, Janai, but that's just plain stupid."

"Look I don't need a fuckin' lecture right now, a-ight? Oh God! Hold on Chanel."

Janai ran to the bathroom and vomited up the ice cream she had just finished. She got a cool rag for her face and cleaned herself up. After she went back to the phone she told Chanel that she was feeling sick and that she would talk to her when she was feeling better.

Chapter 12

Chanel arrived early. She headed for the bar and waited for Donnell. She ordered herself a margarita. As she was waiting she noticed an attractive Puerto Rican man watching her. He smiled and mouthed the word hi. She smiled back and did the same. *Damn he's fine,* she thought. She quickly looked away and continued to sip on her margarita.

The mysterious man went over to sit on the bar stool next to Chanel. Chanel immediately became flushed with anxiety. *Why am I so nervous*? She thought.
"My name is Tony. Tony Velez." She put her hand out for him to shake it and make her acquaintance, but instead he kissed her hand. It immediately sent a warm sensation throughout her body.
"Nice to meet you, I'm Chanel."
"Chanel? I like that. A beautiful name for a beautiful woman."
Chanel noticed an ever so slight, sexy Spanish accent.
"Thank you."
"So Chanel, are you alone?"
"Yes, I mean no, I'm waiting on someone." She was so jumpy she was fumbling her words.

During their mini-conversation they found each other interesting. There was the usual small talk… profession, etc. Tony was planning on moving to Atlanta and inquired about the city. He was a professional baseball player who had been traded from the Marlins to the Braves. And Chanel didn't know the difference because she didn't follow baseball.

"So, Chanel, what do you do?"

"I work for Fox television. I work in the control room. I also cover live shots and overseen the final product before it hits the air."

"Wow! Brains and beauty."

He was impressed especially because she didn't seem interested in his money like every other woman he met. And lately he had been meeting women that didn't particularly have anything going for themselves. All they wanted to know was how much money he made and what kind of car he drove. During their conversation Tony's cell phone rang. He apologized to Chanel. He had to cut their conversation short. He gave her his card with his number on it.

Chanel checked Tony out as he walked away. He had a hard, chiseled body. She could see the outline of his pecs through his fitted silk sweater.

Chanel looked at her watch it was 8:15pm. Donnell was late. *I wonder what's keeping him*, she thought. Just as she was about to call Donnell, he walked up. He didn't feel like hearing her go off on him so he quickly kissed her and then apologized for being late. He said it was unavoidable and he had to finish up with some work at home.

He took her by the hand and lead Chanel to the dance floor where they danced non-stop for about forty minutes. And since dancing can be sensual as well as sexual, they both got each other hot and bothered. Donnell kissed Chanel deeply and passionately.

"You ready to get out of here," he smiled. Chanel nodded. They couldn't get out quickly enough. They got in their respective vehicles and drove towards Donnell's place.

Donnell had all intentions on making love to Chanel, but something changed his mood. He received a message from an old friend from his neighborhood. His friend said he had spoken with Donnell's father and just learned of his mother's death. He offered his condolences.

Chanel came in behind him and shut the door and locked it. She took her overnight bag upstairs to his room. When she came back down, Donnell was sitting on his couch with his face in his hands. He looked distraught.

He got up and pulled his parents' picture off the wall that was adjacent from him. Chanel knew he was still grieving.
"You alright, babe?" She had startled him.
"Yeah, I'm alright. I just can't believe she's gone. That's all." He placed the picture back on the wall and sat back on the couch.

Chanel sat beside him. All she could do was look into his eyes.

"She was a wonderful woman, you know?" Donnell said to Chanel without looking at her. He leaned back on the couch.

"I'm sure. I wish I could have met her." Chanel said sincerely.

"She would've liked you."

"Really?" Chanel sat up in surprise. "How do you know?"

"Just the type of person you are. Not to mention the fact that I spoke about you a few times."

This really shocked Chanel. "What? I didn't know you talked to her about *us*."

"Yeah, she actually asked about you while she was still in the hospital. She referred to you as *'that pretty woman back in Atlanta'*."

"How'd she know what I look like?"

"I had one of your pictures in my wallet when I went home for Christmas last year."

She smiled. "I didn't know you kept a picture of me in your wallet."

Donnell didn't say a word. He just sort of halfway smiled. It was almost as if he didn't want her to know those types of things about himself. He never wanted to be vulnerable to any woman.

Chanel kicked her heels off and laid her head on Donnell's chest.

"I miss her, Chanel."

"I know, but you'll always have the memories. You carry those with you for life."

"You know what? No matter what happens with us Chanel, you gon' always be my girl. 'Cause you got my back."

They sat in silence for a moment. Then Chanel wanted to take his mind off of things for a moment. She told him about Janai being pregnant and that she didn't know who the father was. She practically told her their whole conversation verbatim.

That made Donnell laugh.

"That's a nasty ass, scandalous woman."

They laughed and joked and continued to talk for several more hours until they fell asleep in each other's arms on the couch.

Chapter 13

Janai spent most of the sun up hugging the toilet bowl. The morning sickness was beginning to take its toll on her.

Janai had to rush to get ready for work. She managed to get in and out of the shower in seven minutes and decided to throw on something casual and comfortable. She chose a blue cotton shirt and some matching Capris with a pair of sneakers.

She grabbed some fruit and crackers for the nausea and threw them into her purse. Before she was able to get out of her apartment good, the phone rang. She quickly answered it.

"Hello? Hello? Hellooooo, is anyone there? Look, whoever this is, I don't have time for silly games." Still, nothing is heard. The other party hung up.

"Damn prank callers!" She rushed out the house. Just as she was approaching her car, she noticed that all of her tires were flat.

"What the fuck! Oh, hell no." She looked at her watch. She realized she only had half an hour to get to work. Jordan had already left for work, so she couldn't use his truck. *Damn*, she thought. *Why me? Why now?*

She ran back into the house to call him on his cell phone. It rang five times and his voice mail picked up.

"Shit!" She left a message anyway. "J, it's me. Look all of my tires are flat and I need a ride to work. So, I need you to come and get me."

She decided not to call and let them know at work that she'd be late, just in case Jordan made it to her in the next few minutes and hauled ass to get her there.

She even went to two of her neighbors' apartments, but to no avail no one was home. After twenty minutes had passed she figured she would not make it on time. She called her job and let them know that she'd be a little late.

As she was hanging up, Jordan called to say he got the message and that he would be on his way in the Fed-Ex truck. When he got there, Janai was waiting for him outside. She was already about thirty minutes late, which meant by the time she got there she'd be about an hour late.

On the way there, Jordan inquired about her car. "How in the world did you get four flat tires?"

"I don't know, what kind of stupid ass question is that? It's probably one of those stupid ass, little, ghetto kids, in the next building."

"Well, whoever did it, knew what they were doing because I could tell there weren't any slashes in them. The air was let out slowly."

This got Janai's wheels turning. She thought yet again about Sonya. *No, she doesn't even know where I live; besides, I haven't messed with Robert for over a month now. Couldn't be her messin' with me. Or could it?*

About halfway through Janai's teaching session, Mrs. Dean came into her classroom and told her she needed to speak with her once class adjourned.
Mrs. Dean began, "Ms. Love, you don't seem to understand how hard it is for people to find jobs these days do you?"

Janai didn't say a word.
"Let me spell it out for you. You were already late about a month ago and now you stroll in here today late. You're really treading on thin ice. So, essentially what I am saying is I am putting you on probation effective immediately. One more strike and your contract will not be renewed for the next school year."

"Look Mrs. Dean, I had four flat tires. I only have one car and no other way of getting to work. So, I had to wait for a ride."
"You're supposed to set an example Ms. Love. Not be an example. Our students look up to you, so you

must be on your p's and q's at all times. Your character says a lot to these students. Now if you don't mind, I have a lot of work to do. Good day, Ms. Love."

She never even looked up at Janai when she dismissed her.

Chapter 14

Chanel woke up to find Donnell reading an article from *Black Enterprise*, while eating some fresh fruit. Chanel glanced to her right at the clock on the wall; she still had about an hour and a half to get ready for work.

"Morning sleepy head," Donnell said to her while eating at the breakfast bar.

"Hey." Chanel smiled as she fluffed out the back of her hair.

"You hungry? I got some fresh fruit in the fridge."

"Uh, yeah," Chanel said, still feeling a bit disoriented. "That's probably all I'll have time for anyway.

"Help yourself. It's in the fridge."

"Well on second thought," she said after secretly checking her breath, "I think I'll go and brush my teeth and take a shower first."

While Chanel was in the shower, Donnell returned the call to his friend who had left a message of condolences on his answering machine.

In the shower, Chanel reflected on last night and how Donnell was finally opening up to her. She took this as a sign that maybe he wanted to take the relationship to the next level.

Chanel stepped out of the shower to call in to her job so she could play hooky and spend the day with Donnell. She picked up the receiver on the nightstand, that's when she heard something that knocked the wind from beneath her sails. Donnell was in the middle of a conversation with his buddy from L.A.

"Yeah, man I'm really sorry to hear about your mother. She was like a second mother to me."
"Thanks man. Chanel had my back though."
"Sounds like marriage material to me, Donnell."
Chanel wanted to put the phone down, but changed her mind. She smiled when she thought Donnell was telling his friend good things about her.
"Bite your tongue man. That's never going to happen. I will forever be a bachelor. Besides, after seeing the pain and hurt my father is going through over the loss of my mother, I know I don't ever want to feel like that!"
"Don't you think that's a little extreme? I think it's a beautiful thing…your pops really loved your mom. Man, if you don't do right by Chanel, I'm sure she will leave you and you'll still be left hurting."
"She hasn't so far. Besides she's a smart woman. She should have figured out by now that's never going to happen, not in a million years. Not with me."

"Alright Donnell, I just hope you know what you're doing. Anyway, I gotta go now and you keep it light."

Chanel's smile had disappeared and was replaced by tears. *Never? Not in a million years? I have been such a fool*, she thought. Chanel quickly finished getting ready, grabbed her bag and headed downstairs.

"Hey babe, how was your shower?"
"Fine," she said dryly.
Donnell tried to embrace her and kiss her, but she nudged him away. "Hey, what's wrong?"
"What could possibly be wrong Donnell? I'm late. Goodbye." Chanel hurriedly walked out the door.

Chanel cried all the way to work. Once she got there, she could barely concentrate. She was hurting and needed to talk with someone. She called Micki at work and told her what she overheard Donnell saying.

"I told you. That man was running game on you the whole time, and you couldn't even see it. No, correction, you didn't want to see it. So now what are you going to do since you know the truth?"
"I'm going to confront him and give him an ultimatum."
"What? Chanel that's dumb. Why put yourself through that when you already know the truth?"

"I know, but I need some type of closure if this is how it's going to be."

"No, Chanel, listen to me. All you need to do is leave that nigga alone and take care of you. It'll give you a positive attitude and some self-esteem. Put God first and everything will fall into place."

"No offense Micki, but right now, I don't need a sermon."

"You just wait 'til I talk to that dirty dog."

"No Micki, I'll handle this. It's my business."

"Okay little cuz. Call me if you need me."

This was the first time Donnell had time alone to reflect on his life since his mother's death. He was still deeply hurt by his mother dying. He also felt as if he was abandoning his father, although his father insisted that Donnell go back home and get on with his life.

As for his relationship with Chanel, Donnell had no intentions of taking things to the next level, at least not right now. He cared about her, but that was the extent of it.

Donnell had a busy day. First he was off to the bank to deposit a check, and then he had an all day meeting with some potential clients.

Before leaving home, he called Chanel at her job for the second time. The administrative assistant

answered the phone, "Chanel Jackson's office…
this is Susie."

"Hi Susie, it's Donnell again. Is Chanel free yet?"

"No, she's still busy, Mr. Black."

"Okay well when she gets some free time, have her
call me on my cell."

"Will do, Mr. Black."

Donnell suspected something was wrong, but he
couldn't for the life of him, figure what could be the
problem. He arrived at *B of A*, fifteen minutes later.
Donnell glimpsed at the bank clerk. She was
gorgeous! Her complexion reminded him of
cinnamon toast. She had a head full of micro-
braids. *Sure would like to eat her for breakfast.
Baby's fine* he thought to himself while licking his
lips. The woman's nameplate read, Simone.

"How can I help you today?" Simone said to
Donnell flirtatiously.

As Donnell was filling out the appropriate forms, he
was also flirting. Simone leaned forward while
counting his money out loud. She sported a red
blouse with a v-neck, showing off her voluptuous
cleavage. Simone boldly wrote her number on the
back of Donnell's receipt.

"Call me sometime. You aren't seeing anyone, are
you?"

The half-truths just quickly rolled out of Donnell's
mouth. He told her he wasn't seeing anyone
seriously and that he had a "friend" and that they

were in an open relationship and were both free to see other people.

Simone smiled. "Good, does that mean we can go out sometime?"

"We'll see, Simone." He smiled and walked away.

On his way out the door, Donnell saw Micki getting on the elevator. He waved to her. She did not respond, but just cut her eyes and turned away from him. The door closed to the elevator and Micki was gone. Donnell shook his head in bewilderment. *"What's her problem? Is everyone on their period or something?"*

****

Chanel was not getting anything accomplished at work. All she could do was think about Donnell. Each time he called, she told her assistant to make something up, yet she really wanted to talk to him.

Chanel's private line rang again, *I'm sure it's Donnell, I'm still not ready to talk to him.* She yelled to her assistant, "Susie, just tell him I've gone home for the day."

"It's Ms. Love."

"Oh, ok go ahead and put her through." Chanel was surprised by her disappointment.

"Whaddup, cow?"

"Hey."

"Ugh, what's wrong with you?"

"In a word…Donnell."

"What's he done now?"

Chanel relayed Donnell's phone conversation to Janai. She just listened intently without interruption. When Chanel finished, Janai tore into Donnell.

"I've always told you that you deserve better. He ain't nothing but a lying ass, filthy, mothafuckin' dog. And when you lie down with dogs you wake up with fleas. Now when did you want to go and slash his tires and bash his windows?"

Chanel had to slow Janai down a bit. Ghetto, was definitely not Chanel's style. She told Janai that she intended on having a chat with Donnell that night. Janai felt like all Donnell was going to do was snow her like he always has.

Chanel quickly changed the subject.

"Anyway, so have you made a decision yet?"

"I'll probably have an abortion. I don't want to be anybody's mother."

Although Chanel didn't think her friend should terminate her pregnancy, she also wanted to remain supportive. She told Janai that if she wanted her to go to her appointment with her to let her know. When they finished talking, Chanel called Donnell on his cell phone. He answered on the first ring.

"We need to talk."

"About what?"

"Look, just meet me at my place this evening when I get off work."

"Sure, but Chanel what's this…?" The call was disconnected. Chanel wanted to blind-side him.

She didn't want him to have the opportunity to think of some more lies. She wanted to look him in the eyes when she confronted him.

An hour after Chanel came home, Donnell arrived. She let him in, then ushered him out on the deck.

"So what's this all about Chanel?" Donnell looked curious and worried at the same time. "Why the attitude?"

She ignored his question. "Let me ask you something...What are your intentions with me?"

"What?"

"Where do I stand with you?"

"Chanel, we've had this talk several times. And frankly, I'm tired of talking." Donnell turned his back to her.

Chanel stood up and turned Donnell towards her, "Oh, no mothafucka you gonna talk today!"

Donnell looked at Chanel as if she were a stranger. "Just who the fuck do you think you talkin' to?"

Chanel disregarded his attitude. "Do you have plans to marry me? Ever?"

"Someday. Maybe."

"So, you've actually thought about marrying me?"

He paused. "Yeah."

"No you haven't! Why are you lying? I heard you on the phone this morning."

"What? Were you eavesdropping on my conversation?"

"Don't try to flip the script on me. You're just mad, because you are cold busted."

"Look, I've never lied to you. I've always been frank with you."

"Donnell, I laid everything out and let you know how I felt about you. I even told you that I loved you. And you took advantage of that. You *never* had any intentions of marrying me."

"Chanel, you knew who I was when we met. Besides, I never kept you from seeing other men."

"You just don't get it. It's not about me seeing other men. It's about how I felt when I was with you. I only wanted to be with you."

"Well that was your choice." Donnell gave her a look of disdain.

"You are such an arrogant bastard. I can't believe that I was in love with you."

"Look, you got one more time to call me out my name," he said pointing a finger in Chanel's face.

"Well, Donnell you don't have to worry about me calling you at all."

"Oh, so what, you call yourself breaking things off with me?"

"Yes, as a matter of fact I am. I'm tired of your shit. I'm tired of the lies. I'd rather be by myself than to be mistreated."

"Mistreated? I've treated you very well. I take you to fancy restaurants, buy you expensive gifts, and pay for exotic trips."

"Well to coin a phrase, 'that was your choice'." Chanel countered. "Did I ask you to do any of that? All I ever wanted from you was for you to *love* me."

This was a side of Chanel that Donnell had never seen before. He did not know how to respond to her outburst.

"Now I want you to leave."

"If that's your call." Donnell started walking towards the door. As he opened it, Chanel called out to him.

"Wait! Take these with you." She had a shopping bag full of things that he had bought for her; a sweater, some lingerie, earrings, a bracelet and the Nefertiti necklace and a few other trinkets.

He looked in the bag. "No, you keep them. I wanted you to have them."

"Okay." Chanel's momma didn't raise no fool.

Donnell turned his back on Chanel and slowly walked out the door. As she was closing it, Donnell turned with his head cocked to one side and look at Chanel.

"Look I hope you don't think this is the part where I apologize, because I don't have anything to apologize for."

Chanel shook her head in amazement, but said nothing.

"Well when you change your mind, give me a call."

Don't hold your breath, she said to herself as she slammed the door.

During the course of the next several weeks, Janai's doctor confirmed that she was indeed pregnant. She still had not revealed her condition to Jordan.

Janai stepped out of the shower and stared at her naked body. She noticed her belly had started to poke out just a little. Her breasts had also become tender. She ran her hands in circular motions over her belly.

She shook her head. "Snap out of it," she said out loud to herself. "You know you'd just end up being just like your own mother."

That's it! She had made up her mind. She called the clinic to schedule an appointment for the following week. They explained to her that she had to wait at least a couple of days before they would do the procedure. This gave the mother time to ensure that she was making the best decision.

Jordan entered the room as Janai was getting off of the phone. She quickly grabbed her bathrobe to hide her condition.

"What's up, J?"
"Nothing. I'm tired. That basketball game wore me out. But not enough to forget about you." He walked toward her and tried to untie her bathrobe.
"No, J, I'm tired, I think I want to take a nap."
"What's up with that? You've never been too tired to have sex. But for the last few weeks you been trippin'. What's up?"

"Look I just don't want to do anything alright? Damn, do you always have to think with your dick?"

"You know it's not even like that with me."

"I can't tell." She took that as her opportunity to get away. She went into the living room and laid down on the sofa. *I can't keep this up much longer. He's going to know what's up real soon. I just need to hurry up and get rid of this kid.*

****

During the next few weeks, Chanel had started doing something that she should have done a long time ago. Taking care of herself. She had purchased a treadmill and some free weights and put them in her spare room. She also went out a lot more with the girls. She had decided that she wasn't going to let Donnell get the best of her. She still thought about him quite often, but she refused to allow him to fog her mind. She was dog tired by the time the phone rang. She hopped off the treadmill and grabbed the phone in her bedroom.

Much to her surprise it was Donnell. He told her he was calling to invite her to Mary J. Blige's concert, but what he was really doing was calling to pick her brain so he can get back in those panties. Chanel told him that she already had her ticket and that he would have to invite someone else.

"Do you at least want to hook up after the concert Chanel?"

She was tempted. After all, she did miss him. "No, I don't think so."

"You sure? You sound kind of hesitant."

"Look Donnell, stop trying to pick my brain and play mind games."

"What! You act like we can't even be friends now."

"You took me through five years of bullshit when you knew exactly what I wanted."

"Well, if you just gonna stay stuck on that old shit, then I gotta go."

"Bye," Chanel said rather abruptly and slammed the phone down. She had to get a hold of herself.

Although she realized Donnell was an asshole and he mistreated her, she must admit that she missed his dick. He really knew how to rock Chanel's world. Just the thought of having him in her sent shivers down her spine. To take her mind off of him and the situation she drove over to her cousin's for some one on one talk.

As they sat and chatted for a while Micki told Chanel that she should start going out with other men to see what else is out there for her. And that there were men out there that would treat her like a lady with respect. Chanel had already been thinking about that, but for some reason she always felt like she was cheating even if she accepted anyone's phone number. That was only because her heart belonged to Donnell. But he never reciprocated that.

"Then there's no time like the present Micki," she pulled a napkin from her purse with Tony Velez's number on it. Micki snatched it from Chanel's hand.

"What's this? Heifer you been holding out on me? Who is Tony Velez?"

After Chanel explained who he was and how they had met, Micki was thrilled for her cousin.

"Well, what are you waiting for? Go on and call him."

"No." Chanel wanted to call but she was just nervous. She was used to men approaching and calling her... not the other way around.

"Call him right now."

"Okay. Shush!" The phone was ringing.

"Bueno?"

"Hola!"

"Quien es?" That was the extent of Chanel's Spanish.

"Hi, Tony it's Chanel."

"Chanel? Whoa, I didn't think I was going to hear from you. How have you been?"

"Pretty good. And yourself?"

"I'm just letting my shoulder heal. I injured it during practice. Other than that, I've been great. So, what made you decide to call me after all this time?"

"I was just wondering if you wanted to go out for coffee sometime?" She felt like a schoolgirl. *Out for coffee* she thought. *How stupid I must sound.*

"Coffee, huh?" He snickered. Sure, why not?"

Chanel gave him her number and told him she'd be in touch.

The whole time she was on the phone Micki kept trying to whisper little things for her to say. Chanel in turn kept covering the receiver and telling her cousin to shut up.
Once Chanel hung up, she and Micki were giddy like two teenage girls discussing all the sordid details.

The next day Chanel hung out with Janai and Micki at her place. They gave each other manicures and pedicures and also massages. But mainly, they talked shit. They all sat in Chanel's Jacuzzi out on the deck.

They talked about anything and everything. Then Micki began to inquire what was going on with Janai's world. She told her everything about the pregnancy and that she had scheduled an abortion.

"What?" Chanel looked at Janai suspiciously. "Have you told Jordan yet?"
"No, it's not his business. I'm the one who's carrying it."
"It's his child too and he has a right to know what's going on."

Micki decided to interject. "Look Janai, before you make such a huge decision, why don't you come to church with me. Get some spiritual direction. I invited both of you a while ago. You're still welcome to come anytime."

"Why? Going to church is not going to solve my problems. You know, I never did understand why you people always say, 'go to church', as if it's just going to miraculously solve all my problems."

"I just mean that maybe you could use some guidance to help you make better decisions for your life."

"Who says I'm not already making a good decision?"

"Come on, Janai, think about it," Micki continued. "You were obviously having unprotected sex; you sleep with married men for money. You drive a nice car, but you still have an apartment. Shall I continue?"

The shit had hit the fan. Janai was furious. "For your information, I *do* pray *and* read the Bible. What right do you have to pass judgment on me? You're just like the rest of these so called Christians." Janai gestured quotation marks with her hands.

"You think you're better than me, because you drive a Lexus and got a house? My parents didn't give me everything I wanted. I have had to work for what I want."

Janai's words hit Micki to the core. She wasn't passing judgment, just pointing out to Janai how she might need help with her decision. Micki told her she wasn't handed anything either and that she worked for everything she had and learned how to invest at a young age.

"Well, good for you," Janai replied snidely.

Chanel had to put a stop to this before someone got hurt. "Look will both of you shut the hell up! This is supposed to be a day for relaxation."
"Hey she's the one judging," Janai cried.
"I was only trying to help, Janai. Consider the conversation dropped."
"Good." Janai quickly changed the subject. She inquired when Chanel and Micki were going to the concert.

"The concert starts at seven," Chanel answered.
They all sort of sat in an uncomfortable silence for a moment.
Once again Janai changed the subject. This time she inquired about Donnell. She asked Chanel if he had called or if the two had been creeping with each other on the low. Chanel was giving her the latest on Donnell when her cell phone rang.
"Hi pretty lady."
"Who's this?"
"Oh, so you don't recognize my voice huh?"
"Oh, hey Tony. I'm sorry, I didn't recognize it at first."

Janai frowned and looked at Micki as if to say, 'who's Tony?'

"It's ok. Anyway, I wanted to take you up on your offer to go out for that cup of coffee."
Chanel told him that she had plans to go to the concert with Micki. He told her that the concert didn't last all night and suggested that the two meet somewhere afterwards. He explained that he was calling from his private jet and would be landing shortly. He wanted to know if he could drop by her place to bring her something. Chanel obliged him and gave him directions from the airport.

Immediately upon hanging up the phone she gave Janai the 411 on Tony.
"Wait a minute, hooka, who is Tony?"
"That's her Puerto Rican papi," Micki smiled.
"What? When did this happen? Now *I'm* out of the loop?"
"It's not like that. I just met him a few weeks ago. I'd actually forgotten that I had his number."
"Hookah please. You know you kept that number on retainer. Always have a back up plan. Especially when a nigga wanna act up." They gave each other a high five.

Chanel went to make herself somewhat presentable. She told the girls that Tony should be there in an hour or so. The girls decided to drape themselves in their bathrobes to cover up their swim attire. They wanted to wait to see him. About an hour and a half later Tony called Chanel to let her know that he was downstairs. She buzzed him up. Meanwhile, Janai and Micki peeked outside to see what they could see.

"Damn girl, he's fine! He looks like the Rock."
"Come here Micki. Doesn't he look like the Rock?"
Micki nodded and the girls giggled as they took turns playing voyeurs.
When Chanel opened the door for Tony, both Janai and Micki hurried over to the couch.
Tony handed Chanel a bouquet of flowers. He said he couldn't wait until tonight and he wanted her to have them now.
"Thank you. They're beautiful."
Micki cleared her throat, trying to bring attention to herself and Janai. Chanel swiftly introduced Tony to the girls.
Janai decided to kid Tony a little and inquire if he had any brothers or cousins.
Once they were done with their small talk Tony told Chanel to call him when the concert let out. He said he would have his limo driver pick her up.

Once he had left, the girls all jumped up and down like they were back in elementary school.
"Girl, he's fine and he's a gentleman. Lil' cuz, you better keep him around."

After the concert, Chanel and Micki waited for Tony's driver to arrive. Micki waited with her because she didn't want Chanel standing outside alone at night.

As they were waiting they were talking about how much they enjoyed seeing Mary J perform, Donnell walked by looking for his car. Once he spotted Chanel of course he tried to pour on the charm as usual. He kept trying to coerce her into spending time with him.

"Well, what about tomorrow, maybe we can do breakfast or something?"

"Look, can't you see she's not interested in you," Micki offered as she cut her eyes at Donnell.

Donnell looked at Micki with disgust. "You need to mind your own business. Maybe if you get a man, and get you a life you can stay out of your cousin's."

Before Micki had a chance to respond, the limo pulled up for Chanel. The driver got out and motioned for her. Chanel got in and waved goodbye to Micki.

"See ya later, cuz."

Donnell just stood there with a stupid look on his face. Then he walked towards his car. Micki shot Donnell a wicked smile. "Bye Donnell. Have a *great* night."

Chanel and Tony drove to Stone Mountain Park and watched the laser lights show. They stayed for a short time and eventually went to Tony's hotel downtown, so they could talk some more. They did the usual "getting to know you" conversation. Chanel learned quite a bit about Tony that night. He is thirty-one years old and has never been married, but has an eight-year-old son. Apparently, he was with his high school sweetheart for quite a while, but didn't want to get married. Even after he found out he was having a son, he simply wanted to focus on his career and his son. Tony told Chanel at this point in his life he is open to a relationship with the right woman, of course.

After a while, Chanel was tired and asked Tony to take her home. Tony instructed his driver to bring the limo around and he walked her to the door.

"Thanks for a nice evening, Tony. I really had a great time."

"So did I, pretty lady. I enjoyed your company, too. Just don't make this the last time I talk to you."

"We'll talk again." She gave him a hug and immediately felt chemistry.

It was obvious they had a strong attraction for one another. But Tony remained a perfect gentleman. He kissed her on the cheek and left.

Before Chanel went to sleep, she saw that Donnell had called five times, although he hadn't left a message. She liked the fact that he was squirming and probably wondering what she was doing.

Early the next morning, Chanel was rudely awakened by the telephone. She answered it with a groggy voice. "Hello?"

"Late night, huh?" It was Donnell calling to get all up in her business.

Chanel, however wasn't forthcoming with any information. It wasn't Donnell's business what she did or didn't do with anyone else. So when he didn't get any of the answers he was looking for, he tried to convince her that it was a good idea to allow him to come over for lunch. Chanel, of course, being the main dish.

"I don't know, Donnell. I'm not so sure that's a good idea." Just then, Chanel's doorbell rang. She wondered who in the hell could be at her door this early. She put on her bathrobe and looked out her peephole. It was a deliveryman.

"Yes", she inquired without opening the door.

"I have a delivery for a Ms. Jackson from a Mr. Velez."

Chanel smiled and opened the door. She told Donnell to hold on and sat the cordless phone down and took her beautiful floral arrangement and put them in some water. There was a card attached that read: *Chanel, I hope you like the flowers. This is just a little something to let you know I am looking forward to starting a great friendship with you. Keep smiling pretty lady. Tony*

Oh, that is so sweet, she thought. Chanel was so caught up in her own thoughts, she almost forgot about Donnell.

"Damn, you had me on hold for a minute."

"Sorry."

"What was so important that you almost forgot about me?"

Chanel told him that a floral arrangement had been delivered to her and Donnell put two and two together. Then he started hating on Tony and implying that Tony was only trying to gain brownie points, and that all men do sweet things when you first meet. Then he went on and on about what he's done for Chanel and what he's bought for her. Chanel knew what time it was and knew that he only did those "sweet" things when he thought that he was in the doghouse...not because it was genuine.

Donnell asked Chanel for another chance and he said that although he couldn't change the past he could only work on the future. He convinced her that he would prove it to her.

"So, are you going to let me come over and bring you some lunch or what?"

In her mind, Chanel knew better, but her heart could not resist.

"Ok, Donnell, you can come over around two."

Donnell grimaced. "I'll see you then."

Several hours later the two were all hugged up on the couch in the nude. Donnell had used his charm yet again. He had brought over some Chinese food

111

and a bottle of wine. He even gave her a massage. The rest was history.

"You're going to call ol' boy right?"

"He has a name, Donnell, its Tony. And yes, of course, I'm going to call him and tell him we've gotten back together."

"Good. And you're going to get rid of those flowers right?"

"Wrong. Donnell, he is just a friend and besides they're just flowers. They only last a few days anyway."

"Friends, huh? So, what did you two do?" Donnell sounded jealous.

"What you really want to know is did we have sex, right?"

"Did you?"

"No, Donnell." She shook her head in amazement. She couldn't believe how jealous he was acting. This wasn't like the cocky Donnell she knew.

"Do you honestly think I would play myself like that? I mean it had only been a week or so since you and I had spoken."

"I just don't like to think of you with anyone else, that's all."

"Is that why you're here?"

"I told you. I'm here because I want to be and because I missed you." Then he kissed her passionately and they made love for another hour

Chapter 15

Monday morning came and Janai had passed out the test to her summer school students. She had three more days left and she'd have a break until the end of August.

The students were quiet as they took their test. Janai thought about the appointment she had scheduled for later that afternoon. The plan was for Chanel to pick her up from the school. *After today, it'll be all over*, she thought. While Janai was lost in her trance, a woman wearing shades approached her.

"May I help you?"

"Yes, I need some information."

"Sure, but let's talk in the hallway so my students won't be disturbed. They're taking a test."

"Actually if you don't mind, I'd rather sit down. I'm physically challenged and I can't stand for a long time."

"Ok, but keep your voice to a minimum. What kind of information do you need?"

"It's about my daughter, Sidney."

"I don't think I have any students by the name of Sidney?" Janai said inquisitively thinking the woman might've been a parent of one of her students.

"Sidney doesn't want to go to school anymore and has no interest in other kids her age." Janai listened to the strange, mysterious woman as she talked.

"I'm sorry, but how do you figure I can help you with that?"

"Well, I figured since you're a teacher, that you knew how to handle children and knew what to say to them. You see, Sidney doesn't want to face her peers because she's embarrassed that her father and I are getting a divorce. My husband cheated on me."

Janai was even more confused. "Ma'am I'm sorry, but I just don't know how I can help."

The woman's voice started to escalate. "Let me see if I can clarify it for you. You're the bitch that broke up our happy home!"

The woman dropped her shades and Janai's blood ran cold. She recognized the wife of an old lover.

"Look whatever he told you isn't true. He tried to come on to me, but I resisted."

"Don't lie, bitch! I know everything! He told me!"

By this time her students were all staring at the deranged woman. Janai switched gears.

"Well if you knew how to take care of your man, he wouldn't have come to me in the first place!" Janai retorted.

"You never cared about Robert. I know about bitches like you. You seek out married men. You don't want a commitment, just the money and gifts. It's bitches like you that need to be taught a lesson."

"Look Sonya, you need to leave. These kids don't need to be hearing this."

"I don't think you understand, I'm not leaving…you are bitch!"

"Well, I don't have anything more to say." Janai turned her back to talk to the students. "I need everyone to go wait out in the hall." She tried to escort them all out, but Sonya reached in her purse and pulled out a small handgun.

"Bitch, the only place you're going is straight to hell!"

Only a few students made it to the hall. The others screamed in terror when Sonya produced a gun. Sonya wasn't interested in hurting the children, only Janai. She told them all to hurry up and get out. Meanwhile, Janai had managed to back away from Sonya's focus.

"And just where do you think you're going?"

"Look, I'm sorry about everything."

"Oh, so *now* you're humble? Ain't that a bitch! A few minutes ago you were telling me I didn't know how to take care of my man."

"I didn't mean it. I was angry." Janai had tears in her eyes. "Please just put the gun down."

"No, I think I'd much rather watch you squirm. Just like I did when I waited for Robert to come home at night and he didn't get home until one or two in the morning. Or he'd lie and say he had to work late,

115

but he was really with you. Are you proud of yourself?"

Janai stood there in fear of her life. She didn't say a word. She was trying to figure out a way to get out of this situation. There was only one door.
"Haven't you wondered how I knew where you worked and where you lived? Well, it's easy. I followed you and Robert and I got your license plate number. With that I had all the information I needed thanks to a friend of mine that works at the DMV. But now it's all over." Sonya cocked the gun and aimed it at Janai's chest. Janai pleaded for life. She begged Sonya to put down the gun.

By now, the police had arrived. They had guns drawn and demanded that Sonya drop her weapon.

Sonya took her eyes off Janai for a second. Janai tried to take advantage of this by crouching down low.
"Oh no you don't, bitch!" Sonya screamed at Janai and fired the gun. She missed. She fired a second time. Janai blacked out. She had lost consciousness.

Janai came to in the hospital. Both Jordan and Chanel were sitting on opposite sides of her bed. Janai had been lucky. She had only suffered minor trauma to the head when she fell trying to dodge bullets.

The police in turn had demanded Sonya drop the gun by her feet or risk being shot. She didn't heed to their warnings and they were forced to shoot her in her leg. She was taken to the hospital in handcuffs.

Janai focused her eyes and looked at Jordan and Chanel, she was confused.

"What happened?"
"You're in the hospital," Jordan told her, as he kissed her forehead. It took her a moment, but Janai recalled Sonya and the gun.

Janai wondered just how much Jordan really knew. The look on Chanel's face confirmed Janai's fears. Jordan knew everything. *But if he really did know everything, why would he still be here?* She wondered to herself.

"Janai you gave us a scare. But you know I'll always be at your side." Chanel held her friend's hand as she spoke to her.
"Look I'm going to the cafeteria to get some coffee or something and I'll give you two some time alone." Chanel left the couple. She twisted her head and gave Janai a grimace.

"I'm glad you two are ok," Jordan told her. Janai struggled to sit up in the hospital bed with pillows propped behind her back.

"Who two?"
"You and our son or daughter." Janai could have shit bricks when he said that. *Damn! What else does he know?*
"Janai, why didn't you tell me?

She gave him some story about taking a home pregnancy test and wanting to be absolutely certain of her pregnancy. She informed him that she had an appointment with her doctor.

"How do you know, J?"
"The nurse."
Apparently Jordan was there when they were administering drugs into her system. The nurse inquired if Janai was allergic to anything. After she had run some tests she came back to let him know that they were limited on what they could administer into Janai's system since she was pregnant. They didn't want to do anything to harm the fetus.

"I guess that would explain your sudden weight gain," Jordan said smiling. "Janai I'm excited, aren't you?"

"J, I have to be honest with you, I'm just not ready to be a mother. And frankly I'm not sure if I'll ever be ready."

The smile on his face was replaced with a frown. He tried to reassure Janai that she wouldn't be alone. He would be by her side every step of the way. He was even enthusiastic about two AM feedings and changing diapers. His voice was filled with excitement. And it didn't matter to him what the sex of the child was, so long as they conceived a healthy child.

Janai quickly tried to change the subject. "Enough about this baby talk, when can I get out of this place?"
"The doctor said you can leave tomorrow."
"Good, because I hate hospitals. How did you find out I was here anyway?"
"Chanel called me on my cell phone. Apparently, she's listed as your next of kin."
Janai could hear the hurt in his voice. Then Jordan began to inquire about what actually happened. The police only told him bits and pieces.

Janai gave him some song and dance about some strange woman waltzing into the classroom needing help. And the next thing Janai knew, she was pulling out a gun.

"You didn't know who she was?"

"No. I've never seen her before in my life." Janai lied.

As they continued to talk the on-call physician knocked one time and entered the room. He had come to check her pupils and pulse. He also inquired about her mental well being.

Chanel returned to the room with two cups of coffee in her hands. One for herself and one for Jordan. "Thanks," Jordan said as he took the cup from Chanel.

"Do you guys need some more time? If so, I can wait in the lobby."

"No, it's cool. Actually, I'll leave you two alone now. I need to make a few business calls. I'll be out in the lobby if you need me." Jordan kissed Janai on the forehead.

Once they were sure they were alone, Chanel let Janai know that she knew everything. She told Janai that once she heard from the police about a near fatal shooting, she had figured it out. Chanel was just grateful that her friend wasn't killed.

Janai told her that Jordan already knew because of the nurse, even though, he knew that had not changed Janai's mind or heart. She told Chanel she still wanted to have an abortion.

"How are you gonna convince Jordan?"

"Easy, I'll just tell him. If that doesn't work, I'll lie. I'll make it appear as if I had a miscarriage."

"That's cold, Janai, that's cold."

"Yeah, yeah. All y'all got something to say, but in the end I'll be the one left holding the bag. Alone!"

"Janai, we're your family, we'll help you," Chanel said trying to comfort her friend.

"No, my mind's made up. I'm going to reschedule the procedure."

"Janai, you know I always got your back, but I hope you know what you're doing."

The next day Jordan took Janai home. He took the first half of the day off to take care of Janai and make sure she was comfortable and secure back at home. On the way home he was a regular chatty-cathy. He kept going on and on about the baby. It was baby this and baby that. Then he told Janai he had been up all night because he was conjuring up baby names. If they had a little boy he wanted a Jordan junior or Jordan Michael. If they had a little girl he liked the name Charmaine.

It was driving Janai insane. "Damn it! J, will you please shut the fuck up! Now I didn't want to have to tell you this, but you're getting on my nerves with the baby name bullshit! As soon as we get home, I'm making an appointment to get rid of it."

Janai couldn't have been any colder.

Jordan braked to a screeching halt. "What? You can't do that. Don't I have a say in this? It's my child too!"

"True but, I am the one who has to carry it, which means I have the last say in everything that goes on."

"I can't believe you. You already made the decision. You weren't even going to say anything to me, were you?" Jordan was hurt. He continued the remainder of the drive into the apartment complex.

"You know Janai, you've done a lot of things to hurt me in the past, but this is the worst by far. If you go through with this I'm out."

"What do you mean, you're out?" Janai asked as they were walking into the apartment.

"I mean, I'm leaving. I can't continue to live with someone who would kill a child, especially my child."

She looked at him in his eyes. She knew by the look in his eyes that he was serious. The eyes never lie. She decided to challenge him anyway.

"Yeah, right," she said. Janai picked up the phone to dial the abortion clinic.

Jordan stood there and listened as she made another appointment. He looked at her in disgust and stormed to the bedroom. Janai went after him.

Jordan began taking his clothes out of the closet and out of the drawers and throwing them on the bed. He was livid, but more hurt than anything. If Janai could kill their child he wanted nothing more to do with her.

Janai stormed off to the living room. She didn't want Jordan to leave since he paid all the bills. She knew she'd really need help soon, especially when she would be on vacation for the next month and a half. But she really did not want this child.
While Janai was pondering what she should do, the phone rang.

"Ms. Love?"
"Yes?"
"It's Mrs. Dean."
"Yes, Mrs. Dean?"
"I'm calling about a few things, but first I want to inquire about your health. How are you feeling?"
"I'm fine. Still a bit shaken up, but physically I'm fine."
"Good. The other thing I called about is your employment. Ms. Love, we won't be needing your services after this summer break. Your contract will not be renewed in the fall. You're a liability to this school. A letter will be sent to your residence," Mrs. Dean replied rather curtly.
"What? You have got to be kidding!" "I'm afraid not, Ms. Love. During the last few months you've demonstrated blatant irresponsibility, and yesterday's incident just tops it all."

"What? You're faulting me for that?"

"You pose a liability to this school, Ms. Love, you're not an asset. You could've gotten those children hurt or killed. Not to mention the danger posed to the other staff members."

"I had no knowledge of this woman's intentions until it happened."

"Ms. Love, the police informed me of what happened. The woman confessed that she wanted to kill you because you had relations with her husband. I find that irreprehensible and simply immoral. I'm sure you don't want the parents of your students nor your colleagues to find out how your indiscretion put them in danger. I think it best if you find employment elsewhere for the upcoming term. You needn't come back here. Good day and good luck, Ms. Love."

"Bitch!" She said out loud to herself. Janai couldn't believe how cold Mrs. Dean was to her. Hot tears streamed down her face. She started to panic. Now she would only have a few more checks coming in before she had to pound the pavement to look for a new teaching position in a different district. She had to think and think quickly. She quickly dried her eyes and went into the bedroom. Jordan managed to get most of his things in an old duffel bag. He still had a few items left on the bed.

"Can I talk to you, Jordan?" Janai decided to work her magic as only Janai could.

She told him that she just had a change of heart and that she was scared.

Jordan didn't believe her. He knew part of her decision was based on money and the fact that Jordan took damn good care of her financially. She hardly ever had to come out of her own pocket. He told her he wanted her to call the clinic if she was sincere. He wanted to hear her do it. Much to Jordan's surprise she obliged him. Jordan was ecstatic.

"Don't worry, baby. It'll be alright. You'll see. You don't have to be afraid, I got your back." He picked her up and twirled her around. Embracing Jordan, Janai wondered if she was making the right decision.

Chapter 16

Micki really knew how to throw a party! The weather was perfect, not a cloud in the sky. Music was playing; people were laughing, drinking and having a good time.

It was still rather early, but quite a few people had already arrived. The majority was running on "cp" time, including her cousin. She decided to give Chanel a call to see why it was taking her so long to arrive.

"Girl, where you at?" Micki relaxed her proper talk for her cousin.

Chanel told her that she was preoccupied and would arrive in a half hour or so. She indicated that she was waiting on someone. Micki smiled assuming that it was Tony Velez. Chanel just decided to come out with it and blurted out that it was Donnell who she was waiting on and that the two were back together. Micki, of course, gave her cousin grief, which caused an argument.

"Fine. And what if I said I don't want him in my house, Chanel?"

"Then I would just say you don't want *me* in your house." She told Micki to stop trying to run her life and that she was a grown-ass woman. She made her own decisions and just wanted her cousin to support her no matter what...whether she was right or wrong, and without judgment.

"Fine Chanel, I'll see you when you get here." She hung up the phone. She was furious with Chanel, but she would accept her decision, even if it was the wrong decision.

Thirty minutes later, Donnell walked in carrying a plant and a gift bag. Chanel was walking behind him, trying to interpret the look on Micki's face.

"Hi, Micki," Donnell said with a hint of qualm in his voice.
"Hey," Micki replied matter-of-factly.
"Where should I put these?"
"Well, my guess would be right over there where the rest of the gifts are," Micki answered sarcastically.
"Look Micki, if you have a problem with me, just say so. Don't bite your tongue. Come on let's get it all out."
"Well as a matter of fact Donnell, I do have a problem with you playing my cousin. You may have her snowed, but not me. I got your number. I know how men like you operate. But your time is almost up."
"Is that right?"
"Yes, that is right."
"Here let me take these while you two duke it out," Chanel said. She took the plant and the gift bag and put them with the rest of the gifts.
Meanwhile, Janai and Jordan had arrived.
"Whaddup, cow?"

"Heifer, it took you long enough," Chanel retorted.

"She has her nerve. Don't pay her any attention, because she and Donnell just got here, a few minutes ago."

After everyone greeted each other, Jordan didn't want to waste any more time. He went out back to start the grilling. Donnell and Chanel migrated outside as well, and Micki and Janai stayed in the house talking.

Everyone was having a great time mingling, eating and dancing. Jordan was still on the grill an hour later. Chanel was thirsty and told Donnell she was going to get a wine cooler.

"You want one babe?" Chanel asked Donnell as she was getting up from the lawn chair.

"No, I'll take a real drink. On second thought, it's too hot out here for liquor just get me some bottled water."

On the way inside of the house, Chanel accidentally bumped into a beautiful young lady.

"Excuse me," they both said. Chanel continued to the kitchen. The beautiful young lady went over to Donnell and sat next to him on the lawn chair where Chanel had been sitting.

"Hi," she said.

Donnell's eyes lit up in recognition, she was the woman from the bank.

"Do you remember me?"

Donnell nodded. "It's Simone, right?"

"Right, *Donnell*," she emphasized rather seductively making Donnell blush.

"Look, I'll just cut to the chase. I already know you got a woman, because I saw you two talking. But I think you're fine as hell and all I want to do is fuck you. You down?"

He almost choked on the plate of ribs he was eating.

"No strings, just sex."

"I see modesty doesn't run through your veins," Donnell said regaining his composure.

"I'm very confident. When I see something I want, I go after it. Here, take my card. It has my work number on it as well as my cell. Just think about it."

Meanwhile, Chanel got caught up in conversation with Janai and Micki in the kitchen. Janai went to the sink and looked out the window and saw Donnell and Simone talking.

"Check this out," Janai beckoned to Chanel and Micki. They all peered out the window.

"That ho wants your man."

Chanel rolled her eyes and told Janai that just because you see two people of the opposite sex conversing, that doesn't automatically mean that something is going on.

"Well I'm not stupid and I can read body language real well. That bitch wants your man."

"Janai, you're trippin'. Donnell has changed; give him the benefit of the doubt." Chanel grabbed her wine cooler and a bottle of water for Donnell and went back outside. Micki and Janai followed.

Simone stood up when she saw Micki.

"Hey, Simone what's up?"

"Nothing, just mingling."

"You sure that's all you were doing?" Janai retorted giving her the evil eye.

Chanel handed the water to Donnell. She thought about what the girls said in the kitchen. She didn't want this Simone bitch to think she was mousy.

"Hi, Simone, I'm Chanel," she said as she sat down next to Donnell. She was sure Simone would know what was up.

"Nice to meet you, Chanel."

Simone immediately excused her self, telling Micki she couldn't stay. She said she had a prior engagement and simply wanted to see Micki's house and drop off her gift.

"Okay, see you on Monday, Simone."

"Nice, meeting you all." Simone walked away making sure to shake what her mama gave her.

By now, Jordan had finished grilling and everyone enjoyed his cooking. No sooner than Donnell got up to use the bathroom, Micki's friend John arrived with a buddy. Tony Velez!

John had asked Micki if he could bring a friend but she had no idea it would be Tony. Chanel looked as if she had seen a ghost.

"Tony Velez?! Aw man, can I get your autograph?"

Jordan had recognized him from watching numerous baseball games.

"Sure man."

Chanel became heated. Janai thought the whole thing was funny. She enjoyed the drama.

"This ought to be good," she said out loud.

"What?" Jordan asked her. She filled him in on the details.

"Micki may I speak with you in private?"

Micki knew her cousin was livid, but she didn't care. They walked inside the house and went upstairs.

At least instead of making accusations, Chanel asked her cousin if she was behind this "set up." Had Tony mysteriously popped up?

"I wish I could take credit for this, but I can't. When my friend John said he was bringing a friend, I just assumed it was a woman. I didn't know it would be Tony."

This wasn't much consolation to Chanel. She was a bit upset. She hadn't even told Tony that she had decided to "reconcile" with Donnell. She told Micki to ask Tony to leave.

Micki told Chanel that she would have to do her own dirty work.

"Leave me out of it."

They went back outside. Tony was chatting with Janai and Jordan, enjoying a plate of barbeque.

"Tony, may I speak with you please," Chanel summoned.

"Sure." Before he was able to get up out of his seat, Donnell appeared from the bathroom.

"Chanel babe, I'm tired so let me know when you're ready to leave."

He noticed Tony by her side.

Janai smiled and tapped Jordan on his arm as if to say, watch this.

"Who's this, Chanel?" Tony inquired rather jealously.

"Tony, this is Donnell."

"What's going on? I thought you two called it quits?"

Micki didn't say a word. She just sat and stared.

Donnell recalled that name. "So, this is the dude that got you those flowers and the limo and all that? What's *he* doing here?" He turned to Micki accusingly.

"He came with a friend of Micki's. He didn't know we were back together," Chanel responded.

"Back together?" Tony asked.

Chanel turned to address Tony. "I'm sorry, Tony. It just happened a couple of days ago, and I didn't have a chance to call you and let you know."

"Yeah, so you can just leave buddy," Donnell added.

"Hey man, this isn't your party. I'll leave when she tells me to leave." Tony's Spanish accent thickened.

"Look Tony, I'm sorry, but you and I can't be friends anymore or hang out." Chanel felt guilty.

"I can respect that, Chanel. It was nice meeting the rest of you. Oh, and Jordan…great barbeque!" Tony discarded his empty plate and left.

"Damn!!" Janai had to make her little comments on the side.

Donnell just stood there smiling, content with how everything was going.

"Donnell, I don't know about you, but I'm ready to go." Chanel grabbed her purse and Donnell led her out to the car. She was embarrassed by her actions and by Donnell's gloating.

Chapter 17

Several hours later, Janai and Jordan finally made their way back home.

"Cool barbeque huh, Janai?"

"Yes, I rather enjoyed myself," Janai said as she flopped on the couch. She ran her fingers through her hair and exhaled. "I need a drink. J, will you go pour me a glass of Alize over ice?"

Jordan looked at her like she had bumped her head. He told her that she couldn't have any alcoholic drinks and especially because she was pregnant. He wasn't going to have anyone poison his child or possibly kill it.

And Janai being the person that she is, called him everything but a child of God. She cussed him out like there was no tomorrow. She threatened to fix her own drink if he didn't and she said she'd make it twice as strong, if she had to get up.

Jordan didn't budge.

Janai got up off the couch and walked to the kitchen. She got out a short glass and filled it with ice. When Janai reached for the Alize, Jordan snatched the bottle from her hand. She tried to snatch it back from him. Jordan held tight, which caused Janai to stumble. The bottle fell to the floor and broke.

"Now, look what you made me do," he told her as he went to go get the mop from the bathroom.

Janai was furious and threw the ice filled glass at Jordan. It whizzed by his bald head, he felt the breeze only inches away.

"You son of a bitch!" Janai yelled at the top of her lungs. The glass hit the patio door and shattered. Jordan was stunned.

"Janai, I have put up with more nonsense from you than any man would ever take. You got one more time to pull one of your little stunts and I'm out."

"Whatever nigga! Remember, I'm carrying your child."

"Well just keep on Janai and I'll show you better than I can tell you."

****

When Chanel got home, she had time by herself to think. She felt badly about the way she treated Tony. She had intended on telling him that she and Donnell were back together, but she simply got sidetracked. She mustered up the courage to call him at home.

Tony's conversation with Chanel was completely dry, and rightfully so. Chanel apologized but he wasn't trying to hear it.

"Tony, are you upset with me?"

135

"No…just disappointed. I thought if nothing else, we were friends who could be honest with each other. All you had to do was let me know. I know you said time slipped by, but that tells me a lot. That tells me that you had more important things to do than to give me the heads up. But it's cool. No love lost."

Chanel felt like a heel. She was at a loss for words. Luckily, her call waiting beeped. *Whew*, she thought, *saved by the bell.*
"Can you hold on?" She clicked over and it was Janai calling to get in her business.
She told Janai to hold on while she cleared the other line with Tony. When she came back Janai was all up in her business. She wanted to know what was really going on with her and Tony. And why hadn't Chanel let her know that she and Donnell had hooked back up?

"Chanel, you know Donnell won't change. He'll just be on his best behavior for a few weeks. You know you deserve better."

Chanel went off! She told Janai that she was tired of her and Micki trying to run her life and force their opinions on her. She told her from now on, they need to keep their opinions to themselves, especially if it was negative.

"I understand, Chanel."

"Anyway, let's change the subject. Have you made a decision yet?"

"Yeah, I'm going to have it and J is hype. He can't wait to be a father. That mothafucka has names picked out and shit."

Chanel snickered. "Really?"

"Hell yeah. I'm just not feeling this mommy thing."

"Well, you better get ready Janai…you better get ready.

Janai sighed and thought to herself, *I'll never be ready. Jordan is going to have to raise this kid on his own.* She said her goodbye's to Chanel and hung up the phone.

Chapter 18

When Donnell got home he heard a message from Simone on his voicemail.

"Hi, Donnell this is Simone. I know you didn't give me your number, but I checked in the computer at the bank and got your number. Don't be upset, I won't make a habit out of this, but I just wanted you to know how serious I am. I want you, and I know you want me, I can see it in your eyes. All you gotta do is say the word."

"Damn," he said aloud to himself. "She does have a tight little body. I might need to go on and hit that." He looked in his pocket and took out the business card that she had handed him earlier at the barbeque. He sat for a minute to think. *I wanna hit that, but I don't want to mess things up with Chanel again. I could just sneak, hell she won't know. I'm too careful for her to find out anything anyway. Even if she did find out, I'll just lie. She'll come back to me. Women always say they'll leave their men, but they never do. They're too afraid of being alone.* He stared at the phone number on the card. *Let me at least call and see what's up.*

"Hello, Simone? It's Donnell."

"Donnell," she said devilishly. "I knew you'd call."

"Oh, is that right? How'd you know?"

"I saw how you looked at me and I figured the phone call would push you over the edge, so to speak."

"So basically, you're saying that you set me up?"

"I guess so, if you want to call it that. Enough with the small talk. When are we going to hook up? Tonight?"

"No, not tonight, but soon." He was still undecided.

"Well, you won't regret it, because I got some tricks for your ass."

He got hard just imagining the two of them together.

"I gotta go, but call me when you wanna do the damn thing."

"Okay." He liked Simone's aggressiveness and she had no shame in her game whatsoever. Neither did he.

The next day Donnell and Chanel had spent a wonderful day together. He almost felt guilty about thinking about boning another woman, while he was spending time with another one. After watching a movie on DVD Chanel decided she was tired and wanted to lie down to take a quick power nap. She went upstairs to lie down on Donnell's bed. As soon as she laid her head on the pillow she heard Donnell's cell phone ring. He picked it up before a full ring could complete.

Chanel got a bad vibe, like something wasn't right. She thought Donnell seemed to have fallen back into his old habits. She jumped up out of his bed and decided to stand at the top of his spiral staircase and listen to his conversation. She didn't try to hide either. She didn't say a word, but just stood there with her arms folded.

"Hey, Donnell, it's me Simone. I just wanted to see if we're on for tonight."

"Oh, what's up dawg? I'm just chillin' tonight. Just got in a short while ago," Donnell pretended to be speaking with a male friend.

"Oh, is she there?"

"You know it, dawg."

"And I take it she's standing right next to you?"

"Oh, fo' sure!"

"Well I guess I'll let you go then."

"Alright then dawg, holla back."

"So, who was that?" Chanel asked suspiciously.

"Just a buddy of mine."

"Who? What's *his* name?"

"You don't know him."

"Donnell, I hope you're not up to your old tricks again."

"What old tricks?"

Chanel rolled her eyes at him. "Don't play with me nigga. You don't want to cross me."

She slammed the door to the bedroom. As she drifted off to sleep she wondered if she had made the right choice. Chanel couldn't take it if Donnell was up to his cheating ways again. She didn't want to be hurt again, especially by Donnell. She expected so much out of him. So, for him to do her wrong it would simply rip her heart out. She thought some time away from him would do her a world of good. This would give her time to reflect on what it is she really wanted. She thought a mini-vacation would be in order. Go some place with just the girls. Las Vegas was the perfect place to do just that.

Chanel called Micki and then Janai on three-way. Janai knew she couldn't afford a ticket on such short notice, especially on a teacher's salary. She hadn't told anyone her contract wouldn't be renewed, nor had she tried to find employment at another school. Janai was not the least bit worried. She knew she would get the money from one of her "men". She contacted three people and the last was a success. She got a hold of Steve, another teacher, she used to work with. Somehow, she managed to convince him that she had an emergency and he needed to wire her the money that same afternoon. Steve bought it, hook, line, and sinker.

The night before their trip, Donnell asked Chanel for a favor. He asked her if he could stay at her place while she was away. Apparently, he was having his loft re-painted. He could very easily stay at a hotel but he figured he could stay at Chanel's. Chanel obliged him.
"Thanks, babe, and you ladies have fun, but not too much fun."

The next day, Chanel, Janai and Micki took a non-stop flight from Atlanta to Las Vegas. After they checked in to their hotel, they were famished. They decided to go to one of the midnight buffets. Afterwards, they were so stuffed they had to walk it off on the strip. Janai had become rather tired due to her pregnancy, so she decided to go back to the room early to lie down. Micki and Chanel continued down the strip and played slot machines well into the wee hours of the morning.

The next day Chanel received a call on her cell phone. She noticed a familiar number from the station. Chanel frowned. She wondered what they wanted. She reluctantly answered the phone.

"Chanel, hi it's Monica. We've got an emergency here at the station and we need your help."

"I'm on vacation. Can't you guys find anyone else to help?"

"No, the station manager said she wanted the best person on the job, and that would be you. Not to mention you're the only one available for weekend coverage. I already checked the flights for you. You can be on the next flight in a few hours. It leaves at four."

"Fine, tell them I'll be in tonight." Chanel was disappointed that she had to cut her trip short."

****

It was late evening when Chanel deplaned. After she retrieved her luggage, she searched for her car, which took about ten minutes. She had forgotten where she had parked. Before she drove away, she called the station to let them know she was on the way.

"Oh, we're fine now Chanel. We got someone to cover for you, so you don't have to come in after all. Sorry."

That's just fucking great, she thought. *A goddamn phone call would have been nice.*

"Okay, thanks Monica."

"Ain't that a bitch!" Chanel snickered. "Oh well, at least I can spend time with Donnell."

When she got inside her condo, the lights in the living room were dimmed. But she noticed the lights in the bedroom were on and some music was playing. She called out to Donnell, but she went unheard. *He must be in the shower*, she thought.

Chanel placed here keys on the coffee table in the living room and left her bag near the sofa. She crept down the hall and couldn't believe what her eyes witnessed. Some butt naked woman with braids straddling Donnell. He had one of her voluptuous breasts in his mouth, sucking like a newborn baby.

Donnell was too distracted to notice her. Chanel backed away out of their sight and moved towards the kitchen to grab the largest butcher knife she could find. Chanel proceeded back to her bedroom and slammed the door, she didn't want anyone to get away.

"Just what the fuck is going on!"

The woman jumped off Donnell and turned to face Chanel.

"You're the bitch from the barbeque. Simone. right?"

All Simone could do was stare at the large knife.

"Bitch answer me!"

Simone drew back. "Yes."

Chanel turned toward Donnell, who had managed to back himself into a corner.

"And you mothafucka, I just can't believe you would stoop this low. I mean this is a new one, even for you. You brought this bitch into my home, and in my bed."

"Chanel, it's not what it looks like," Donnell said convincingly.

"Oh nigga don't play me for a fuckin' fool! I will cut the shit out of you if you insult my fuckin' intelligence like that again!" Chanel was waving the knife in his face and yelling at the top of her lungs. Then she lunged at Simone. Simone scrambled across the bed.

Chanel lunged at her again and tried to stab her, but missed. Instead she sliced a part of her own mattress getting the knife stuck.

"What the fuck is wrong with you, Chanel?" Donnell grabbed the knife out of the bed to keep Chanel from hurting or killing someone.

She ran up to Donnell and punched him in his nose. His head rocked back. He was stunned by Chanel's strength. "Oh shit!" Donnell grabbed his nose and tried to focus. Chanel had hit him so hard, he was seeing stars.

Chanel saw that Simone had opened the bedroom door and was trying to head out of the condo. "Oh no you don't, bitch!" Chanel grabbed Simone by her synthetic braids and snatched her back into the bedroom.

Simone fell, face first onto the floor. She tried to sit up but Chanel's street side came out and she started kicking her in the stomach and then she was bashing her head into the wall. "That'll teach you to mess with another woman's man, bitch!"

The next thing she knew the police were at her door. Chanel opened to door in total disarray. Her face had perspiration on it and her hair was a mess.
"Yes, officer?"
"We got a call from one of your neighbor's about a possible domestic disturbance. Is everything alright in here?"

Chanel gave a cunning smile. "No, it isn't officer. I have two intruders in my home, and I want them arrested. My ex-boyfriend is in the bedroom and I don't even know who the bitch is in the hallway."

"You didn't invite either of them, ma'am?" He asked her suspiciously.

"No, I just flew home from Vegas. And there's my suitcase and ticket to prove it. I came home and found them in my home, in my bed."

He passed by Simone who was still sprawled out in the hallway, naked. "Ma'am, were you invited here?"

"Yes."

"Not by me she wasn't."

"Donnell said that Chanel would be out of town for the weekend and that I should come over."

"So you knew when you came over here, that it was not his place."

"Yes, but…"

He cut her off real quick. "I'm gonna have to place you under arrest, ma'am."

"What? Why? I didn't do anything," Simone shrieked. She tried to free herself from the cop's grip.

"Ma'am if you don't stop, we'll add resisting arrest to your charges." He grabbed a blanket off the bed to cover up her nakedness.

"Charges? What am I being charged for?" He ignored her and read her the Miranda rights.

Chanel sucked her teeth at Simone and said to her so as the cop wouldn't hear, "bet you won't fuck with no one else's man."

Donnell was walking out of the bedroom in his boxers. He was still slightly disoriented.

"Is this the other intruder, ma'am?"

"Yes it is."

By this time, the other officer had arrived and assisted with the arrests. "Cuff him while I watch this one."

"Officer, I am not an intruder. She said I could stay here for the weekend while my loft was being painted."

"Is this true, ma'am?"

Chanel shook her head. "I have no idea what he's talking about, officer."

Donnell was angry. "Well if I gotta go to jail, then you all need to arrest her for assault. She hit me in my nose."

"Yeah and she kicked me in the stomach and hit my head into the wall," Simone interjected.

"Officers, the lights were off when I entered my home and when I saw two intruders, I defended myself."

The police officers allowed Simone and Donnell to get dressed then placed them in the back of the police cars.

When all of the excitement died down, Chanel cried for what seemed like an hour. She replayed the scene over and over in her head. It made her so sick to her stomach that she started vomiting.

Unfortunately, she was unable to make it to either the toilet or the trashcan.

After Chanel cleaned up herself and the mess, she stripped the linens off the bed and then she managed to drag her mattress out to the elevator. She'd call in the morning to have it removed. When she got back inside she put everything that reminded her of Donnell in a plastic bag, as well as the sheets from the bed and took it on the deck and burned them in the grill. When she was done she was still angry and hurt.

"No, fuck this," she said out loud. "I'm not gonna let him off the hook that easily. That bastard's gotta pay for playin' with my heart and my life! It's on now."

Chanel needed some sleep. Just as she was reaching to turn out the light in the guest bedroom, the phone rang. It was Donnell.

"Why did you have me arrested?"
"Nigga, you got yourself arrested." She couldn't help but allow her emotions to show. She had loved this man for five years and yet he thought of her as a joke.
He gave her nothing but excuses as to why he did what he did. Chanel wasn't trying to hear it. Blatant disrespect. That was the ultimate. She felt like such a fool to ever believe that Donnell would actually

change. She never felt loved by Donnell, not even once. She was just afraid of being alone and starting over and lost sight of what was important. Herself.

Tears flowed down her face as she spoke to him. She told him that he also lost sight of what was important. Or rather, what should've been important to him. And that was that Chanel supported him wholeheartedly and she stood by him through some rough times.
Chanel had said her peace and was ready to hang up and Donnell sensed it.

"Wait! Please don't hang up."
"Why shouldn't I?"
"I have something to say first. Chanel no matter what you think, I want you to know that I do love you and I have for a while, I was just afraid I'd be losing out of something if I was with one woman."
"Well you don't have to worry about losing out on anything, anymore. It's completely over Donnell. I mean, I'm done." She shook her head.
Donnell pleaded with Chanel to give him another chance.
"I've been doing that for too long now Donnell. You don't get anymore chances."
With that she abruptly hung up the phone.

Chanel wanted revenge and thought of the sweetest way to redeem herself. She remembered Donnell mentioning that one of his neighbors had a spare key to his loft. She worked her magic with the neighbor and let herself into Donnell's place.

She ran upstairs to Donnell's study and turned on his computer. She deleted file after file, erasing Donnell's client list and projects. Chanel found Donnell's laptop and deleted everything on that as well. She ran magnets over his back-up disks to render them unreadable.

Chanel decided his place needed to be cleaned just a little bit. She went into the bathroom and put a stopper in the tub. She let the water run. "Hope he's got insurance, 'cause it's about to be some major water damage up in here." She smiled.

She walked quietly downstairs and ransacked his CD collection. She broke every CD he had except for his Tupac CDs. She loved Tupac. After all what's not to love.

Chanel knew she was being too extreme, but extreme circumstances called for extreme measures. *Revenge is so sweet*, she thought. On her way home, she pumped Tupac's,
'*So Many Tears*'.

Chapter 19

The next day Chanel didn't do much of anything except mope. She stayed in bed practically the whole day and flipped through the channels. She hadn't even bothered to comb her hair, nor had she showered.

Around six that evening Micki called to tell her about the rest of the trip. She was giving Janai a ride home from the airport. Micki knew right away that something wasn't right with her cousin. From the way she so dryly answered her phone and even her answers were short. Chanel wasn't her usual spunky self. Micki tried to pull information out of her, but Chanel was being very evasive.

"Chanel, I'm not hanging up this phone until you tell me what's wrong."
Chanel took a deep breath. "When I got home I found Donnell in my place with that bitch Simone."
"Oh hell no!" Micki decided to put her on speaker phone so Janai could hear, too. As she did that she repeated what Chanel had told her, to Janai.
"What!"
Chanel knew that they both had her best interest at heart, but she didn't have the energy to go over the details.
"See Chanel, I told you that bitch was after your man. I knew it. I could just tell. And that bitch had the nerve to be up in your house?"

Micki wanted to know the details. Chanel recounted what she had seen and how she reacted. Micki gasped in disbelief.

Janai thought it was funny. "You should have cut that bitch. She deserved it," Janai howled, forgetting her own experience with an emotionally scorned woman.

"Don't worry Janai, I got them good. But to make a long story short, the police came and I had them arrested for intrusion. Donnell is still in the county jail."

"Good that's what he gets. Well let's go and do some damage while he's locked up. I may be pregnant, but I'm still down for whatever."

That made Chanel laugh. "No, I already got a little revenge of my own." She told them what she had done to his loft.

Micki covered her mouth in shock. Janai simply cheered her on.

"That's what I'm talking about. That nigga deserved it. All the shit he's been putting you through. It's about time you raised up."

"Well, just for the record, I'm through with Donnell in case you guys couldn't tell."

"Good. You deserve way better."

"Yeah, you were too good for him anyway. And as for that heifer Simone, I'll deal with her when I get back to work."

"What are you going to do, Micki?"

"Let me worry about that right now. I'll handle it and then I'll let you know what went down."

Micki had some unfinished business to take care of the following Monday evening. After everyone in the office had left for the day, she told Simone to come by her office for a little chat.

Simone was wearing a professional burgundy skirt suit. She had her micro-braids pulled back into one big French braid. On the whole she looked quite respectable, but this façade did not fool Micki, she knew the real Simone.

"You wanted to see me Ms. Jackson?"
Micki motioned for Simone to sit in the chair adjacent from her desk.
She didn't drag her feet on the reason why she wanted to speak with Simone. Nor did she sugarcoat anything. Micki fired Simone, on the spot.

"What? Why?"
Micki told her that the state of Georgia was a 'right to work' state. Basically what that meant is that she didn't need a reason to fire her.

A tearful Simone tried to lash out at Micki and accused her of only firing her because of her "crazy cousin".

Micki told her she could do whatever she wanted, but that there were fabrications found on her resume.

Simone was dumb-founded. She didn't quite know what to do or say. Micki sensed this and wanted to get on with her day.

"Just go out there quietly and grab your belongings. A security guard is waiting to escort you out. Now have a nice day."

Simone gathered her things and exited the building unceremoniously.

Later Micki called Chanel and told her what went down.

"What about your job now, Micki? Can't you get fired for that?"

"I'm not worried. Everything I said to her was the truth."

Chanel let out a sigh, "I'm glad this is over. I just need some time to myself. I'm not even going to date right now."

Micki ignored her and completely changed the conversation. She had something else on her mind.

"Chanel I have to tell you something. Something is wrong with your girl, Janai. She's messed up in the head."

"What do you mean?" Chanel was concerned.

"After you left Vegas, we were hanging out at a few clubs and some of the casinos and she ordered a beer."

"What?" Chanel couldn't believe her ears.

"Yeah, and then when I said something about it, she got offended."

"If she keeps it up, she's going to lose that baby."

"Maybe she doesn't care, Chanel. Maybe that's her plan. Remember Jordan is the one who wants it, *not* Janai."

"Thanks for telling me. I'll have a talk with her."

After Chanel hung up the phone she thought about Janai. Would she really try to harm her baby?

Donnell returned home from jail to find his loft a wreck! The upstairs walls had major water damage from the still-running water from the upstairs tub. The carpet was drenched. A wet, mildew odor saturated the air.

"Whew," Donnell cried out shaking his head. He couldn't believe the lengths that Chanel had gone through. He was livid! This was definitely going to cost him a small fortune between repairing and remodeling.

Donnell continued to survey the damage caused by Chanel's wrath. He could not believe that she could get this ghetto. He turned on his computer to retrieve his client list to re-schedule some meetings, and that's when he learned that Chanel had deleted all of his files. This was to low! Even he didn't deserve this.

Donnell dialed Chanel's number. "Don't you think that was a bit much Chanel?" He really wanted to curse her out, but he knew deep down inside he had brought everything on himself. He knew he was dead wrong for his actions. But right now he was more concerned with getting everything fixed and salvaging anything for his business.

"What are you talking about, Donnell?" Chanel asked trying to sound innocent.

"Don't play coy with me, this damage will cost me a fortune to repair. And none of this would have happened if you hadn't been trying to sneak up on me anyway."

"Don't flatter yourself, Donnell. I only came home because of some kind of crisis at work. Imagine my surprise when I saw you suckin' that bitch's titties! Why did you do it? You know what, never mind. It doesn't even matter anymore."

"Well, all I know is that I never would have guessed that you'd be capable of something like that, not to mention chasing that girl with a knife."

"You pushed me to the extreme. Let this be a lesson learned. I'm tired of talking, I need to go." Chanel abruptly hung up the phone.

By now, Janai had now been out of work for about two months. She had sent out her resume to other schools, but to no avail, she had not heard a word from anyone. She had become very frustrated and on edge.

It was the weekend and Jordan had just come home from working overtime. It was rare for him to work on weekends, but with a child on the way, Jordan wanted to save as much money as he could. He kicked his boots off, and picked through the mail. He noticed Janai balled up on the couch.

"Hey babe, are you alright?"
Janai nodded. Jordan tossed the mail on the coffee table and kissed Janai on the cheek and headed for the shower.
Janai picked up a piece of mail marked urgent. She had received a letter from the company that her car was financed through. It read:
To Janai Love,
This is the third invoice we have sent. Yet we have not received your payment. It is imperative that you respond to this notice, as your account is delinquent. Otherwise we regret to inform you that we will have to repossess your vehicle. Please pay now.

Sincerely,

Terry Bolden

"Damn that Robert! He said he would pay for this car, and like a dumb ass, I had him put it in my name. Well, I'm just going to have to give him a call."

Quickly remembering her near death experience she decided to hit him up on his cell phone. She didn't want to risk his wife picking up at home.

As soon as he picked up the phone he got brand new on Janai. He acted as if he didn't remember who she was. Of course with Janai's attitude, all that did was infuriate her and she cursed him out as only Janai could.

"Let me just cut to the chase, Robert. I got a late notice about the car that you're supposed to be paying for."

He flipped the script on her and cursed her out for a change. Janai was shocked. She didn't quite know what to say. She wasn't prepared for this. Robert called her everything, but a child of God. He said the experience had taught him a lesson. He was going to watch out for gold digging tricks.

"The bank is closed! You got it?! You're cut off! Don't ever call here again," Robert said abruptly as he hung up on Janai.

"What! No, he didn't!" Janai slammed the phone down. "Shit!"

Jordan came out of the shower with a towel around his waist. "What are you in here shouting about?"

"Nothing."

Janai quickly switched gears. She told Jordan that she needed some money because she was late on her car payments.

"How much?"

"Twelve-hundred."

He told Janai that he was trying to save money for the new addition to their family and couldn't swing that much. He said he could give her about five hundred dollars. Then he questioned her about being behind on her payments.

Janai had not told Jordan about her work situation. Even with that, Janai had poor money management skills. She finally broke down and told him about getting fired and that she would only be getting two more checks.

Jordan stood his ground. "Janai, we can't afford that right now. I have a truck so it's not like we don't have transportation. Now five hundred is all I can do right now."

"I'm tired of your broke ass, J! You're the only man I know, who never has any money."

They were on a tight budget and she knew that. Jordan didn't care if she cursed him out right now. He did however, care about his baby. He was simply putting his child first, even before it was born.

Janai was steamed. She was about to curse him out when her phone rang. It was Chanel. She was calling to invite Janai to lunch, her treat. She wanted to catch up with her friend, since they hadn't spoken in a while.

"Meet me at the Ruby Tuesday's in Fayetteville in about an hour."

"See ya then," Janai told her.

Janai arrived earlier than Chanel and decided to order an appetizer to hold her over. She was still reviewing the menu when the server approached the table.

"Yes, I'd like to order some cheese sticks and a vodka and cranberry."

The female server looked down at Janai's stomach and then up at her eyes. Janai noticed and became offended.

"Do you have a problem with waiting on me? If so, I can ask the manager to get it for me."

"No ma'am, coming right up."

The server quickly came back with her drink and cheese sticks and Janai had quickly gulped it down before Chanel walked in the door. The two friends hugged each other and began chatting away.

Chanel told Janai that she had simply gotten caught up and lost in her so-called "relationship" with Donnell. She always felt the need to be with a man. She ignored all the warning signs and always felt as if she couldn't do better. But now she's reclaimed her strength and re-validated her own self-worth.

As the two women were talking, Chanel noticed that Janai seemed preoccupied. They were interrupted by the server who had come to take Chanel's order.

"Girl, what is on your mind, 'cause I don't think you're paying attention to anything I'm saying."

Janai looked up and smiled. She realized that her mind must've been elsewhere.

"Sorry."

"Don't be sorry. Just talk to me. What's on your mind?"

"A lot of things. I'm all messed up, Chanel. I was forced to "resign" right after that bitch tried to kill me. I haven't been able to find a school that will accept me this fall. I think that bitch, Mrs. Dean, blacklisted me. And let's face it; no one is going to hire a pregnant woman."

"Why didn't you tell me?"

Janai shrugged her shoulders. She told Chanel she didn't think she was going to need help. She was used to landing on her feet, but fell face first. Janai also told Chanel that the car would be repossessed in two weeks, if she didn't come up with the twelve hundred dollars.

"Damn Janai, we're supposed to be girls, you should have come to me if you needed some help."

"I know." Janai answered softly with her head down.

"Does J, know?"

Janai nodded her head.

Chanel said she would still check her finances, to see what she could do. Janai appreciated that, and knew that her friend was sincere. She felt relaxed.

"What about that *other* thing, Janai?"

"What other thing?"

"The child's paternity? Does J know he might not be the father?"

"Nope and I'm not even going to tell him. There's no need now. He thinks he's the father, so I'll let him believe it, no matter what."

"Janai, that's wrong. That child has the right to know who its father is."

"Its father is whoever I say he is. Besides, you know J believes whatever the hell I tell him."

The server had come back after their lunch and asked if they wanted dessert or coffee. Chanel declined. Janai said that she wanted another vodka and cranberry.

"Um, wait a minute," Chanel told the server. "Don't get that for her, can't you see she's pregnant," Chanel scolded.

The server looked nervous, recalling Janai's attitude earlier.

"Janai, what is wrong with you? You're five months pregnant. You are harming your baby."

Janai was starting to feel the effects of the glass she had earlier.

"A little bit of juice won't hurt the baby."

Chanel wanted to slap Janai. "I can't believe you!"

"Well, believe it." Janai turned to the server, "Don't just stand there. Go get my damn drink."

Chanel read the server's nametag. "Ah, Louise is it?"

The server nodded.

"I'm paying for everything and I don't want that on my check. So the young lady will be having water instead."

Louise quickly walked away.

Janai rolled her eyes at Chanel. "Oh, it's like that, huh?"

"Yeah, it's like that Janai. I'm not going to pay for you to be drinking and hurting your baby."

"Whatever Chanel. Miss high and mighty, never do nothing wrong in her life." Janai was irritated.

"I never said that I didn't make mistakes, but we're not talking about me, we're talking about you and an unborn child's health. So you can be mad at me all you want."

Janai reached into her purse for three dollars and threw it on the table.

"What's this for?" Chanel questioned.

"The tip. Thanks for nothing, *friend*." Then she pushed her chair away from the table and stormed out of the restaurant.

When Janai walked in her apartment, Jordan was on the phone, but quickly got off once he saw her.

"Who you been talkin' to that you gotta jump off the phone as soon as I come through the door?"

"I'll be asking the questions today. Sit down, we need to talk." Jordan was very abrupt with her. Janai also noticed a tone she hadn't heard before.

"What do you want J, I'm tired?"

Jordan just came out with it. "Whose child are you carrying?"

"Excuse me? How dare you ask me some shit like that? Nigga, it's yours, who else would it be?"

"I don't know that's why I'm asking." He stared at her. "Let me rephrase the question. Is it possible it could be someone else's?"

Janai was caught off guard. "Baby, you know you're the only one I want. Why are you even questioning this?"

Jordan began yelling at the top of his lungs. "You lying tramp!"

Janai's eyes got big. Jordan jumped up and walked towards the kitchen.

"Come here, Janai!"

She moved slowly toward the kitchen, but didn't get too close. She had never seen Jordan like this and was extremely nervous.

"I want you to hear this on the machine." Jordan pressed play on their answering machine. Janai heard part of the conversation that she had earlier with Chanel. She realized she had accidentally dialed home while she and Chanel were at lunch. She felt ashamed and embarrassed. But mostly she was pissed off that she got caught.

Jordan was livid. He couldn't even look at Janai. He wanted to strangle her. He took care of her and this is how she repaid him, by sleeping around and without protection obviously. "So who is he, Janai? Who's the other man?"

Janai had no alternative but to confess everything. She told him about Robert Hall and the affair and how his wife, Sonya, was the person who actually tried to kill her.

Jordan was beginning to understand everything now. Now it all made sense…the calls in the middle of the night, the hang-ups, the flat tires. He realized his whole relationship with Janai had been a sham from the beginning. He was simply a pawn in her game to get ahead in life.

"Un-fucking-believable." Jordan shook his head and threw his hands in the air. "I gotta give it to you Janai, you played me. But the joke's gonna be on you if the DNA doesn't come back with the right results." Jordan went into the bedroom and slammed the door.

After a few hours, Jordan was still locked in the bedroom. Janai had not tried to talk to him. She was trying to think of a way to get out of the situation. But she couldn't. She was cold busted and she knew it. There wasn't a damn thing she could say. Finally the bedroom door opened.

Jordan appeared in the living room with two suitcases and a duffel bag.

"What are you doing?"

"What I should've done a long time ago...leave your triflin' ass."

"What? You're going to abandon your child?" Janai was worried.

"I don't have proof that the child is mine. Don't fret, if it turns out to be mind, I'll take care of it. That's the type of man that I am. But that doesn't mean I have to stay with you." Jordan looked at Janai with repulsion. "I can't even stand to be in the same room with you, Janai. Let alone, live with you. So, consider yourself lucky that's it's the first of the month right now and the rent is already paid. You got at least twenty nine more days to find another sucker to pay the rent for you."

With that, he grabbed his things faster than Clark Kent could turn into Superman.

Chapter 20

Donnell had not spoken to Chanel in a month and he really missed her more than he thought he would.
He had saved enough to live off of until he re-established his clientele. One month or so of re-organization didn't hurt him. However, he did lose a few of his clients due to Chanel's shenanigans.

While cleaning up his office at home, Donnell pumped one of his CDs that Chanel didn't destroy. He had left an old Blackstreet CD in the truck. As he shredded papers and alphabetized his files, he remembered how much Chanel helped him when he first got started with his own business. He thought about all the fun they used to have and their lovemaking. This made him smile.

He also remembered how she stood by him when his mother died. Chanel had wanted to be with him, but his male ego wouldn't allow her to see him that vulnerable. But deep down inside, he knew he wanted her there. He was just afraid. Donnell turned down the volume on his stereo and called Chanel.

"Hey Chanel, it's me."
"Me who?" Chanel was giving him a hard time.
Donnell said he wasn't calling to hold her up, he just wanted to call to let her know he was thinking of her.
"That's nice." Chanel was standoffish.

"Why you sound so cold?"

"Oh, do I? I don't mean to sound that way," she said with a sarcastic tone.

"You hate me now, don't you?"

"No, Donnell. I'm beyond that now. Hate actually requires more energy that love. I don't have time for either."

"Why are you talking like that Chanel?"

"Like what?"

"All impersonal and whatnot, like we never had a history with one another."

Chanel chuckled. "Oh, so now we have a history, huh? That's funny."

"Why is that so funny? We *do* have a history."

"Yeah, you're right. It's a history that I would just like to forget and never repeat."

Donnell disregarded her comment. "Look Chanel, I just wanted you to know that I really miss you." Donnell waited for a response. All he got was silence followed by a dial tone.

Donnell was a little upset that Chanel had hung up on him. Normally he would have been running game, but this time it was for real. He meant what he said. He was starting to feel like she was his soul mate. *Would he ever get another chance to make things right?* He wondered.

∎∎

Chanel just couldn't take talking to Donnell another minute. She felt herself weakening when Donnell said he missed her. She did not have enough courage to respond to him, so she hung up the phone.

Chanel knew she had not gotten over Donnell, but she refused to let him back into her heart. Donnell was her drug and she was the junkie. She had to be strong and stand by her decision.

Chanel started cleaning her house to take her mind off of Donnell. When she had almost finished cleaning, the phone rang. Chanel answered it hesitantly. She thought it might've been Donnell again.

To her surprise it was Tony. He was calling to invite her to dinner. She told him it was okay since she and Donnell were no longer together. Tony inquired as to what happened, and Chanel simply told him, without going into detail, that Donnell took her for granted.
She agreed to go to dinner with Tony, but not before she let him know that she was not at all interested in a relationship with anyone at this point in her life. She didn't know what his intentions were, but she wanted to lay everything out on the table.

When the two of them met for dinner, Chanel felt relaxed with Tony. He didn't pressure her to do anything. Who knows where this would lead, but for now it was just a great time, which was all that Chanel wanted.

Chapter 21

Janai was in financial distress. Two months had passed and still she had not found a job. She had exhausted all of her possibilities of getting her hands on some more cash.

Robert was a no go. She tried calling Steve, but learned that he had moved and had an unpublished number. She tried her other boy toys as well, but they simply were unable to help.

Janai had less than three hundred dollars in her checking account and zero in savings. She did not have enough to cover her seven hundred dollar rent, let alone the now sixteen hundred dollars she owed on her car.

Since her car was in repossession status, Janai would simply park down the street from her apartment complex and walk the rest of the way home. This had started to become tiresome to her since she was in the last month of her pregnancy.

However, today she felt ill after returning from her prenatal appointment, so she took a chance and parked in her regular spot at her complex.

There was a knock at her door. Janai got up and looked out her peephole and recognized one of the managers from her complex. She ignored the door as the manager kept knocking. Finally he left a piece of paper in the door and walked off.

When he left, Janai opened her door and grabbed the notice off her door. It read:

PLEASE PAY IN THE AMOUNT OF $700.00 PLUS A LATE FEE OF $50 BY OCTOBER 15TH OR VACATE THE PREMISES!

Shit! Why is this happening to me, she thought.

Janai's answering machine was blinking indicating she had unheard messages. She pressed the play button. There were several messages from Chanel. She did not return any of the calls, she was still mad at Chanel. Instead, Janai called Jordan. He answered his cell phone rather urgently.

"Hello?"

Janai didn't say a word. She simply hung up. She felt too ashamed and embarrassed by what she had done to him to ask him for anything. She felt like she was too good for public assistance. She still had a little time left to play with before she was evicted.

All this thinking had made Janai hungry. Nothing in the fridge seemed to tempt her tummy. She decided to go to the store and pick up something quick to put together. She put on her lightweight jacket and grabbed her keys and purse. As she was locking her door she noticed a tow truck about to latch on to her car.

"Wait!" She was yelling at the top of her lungs and tried her best to run, but her stuffed belly slowed her down. When Janai finally met face to face with the men who were taking her car, she was out of breath.

"What the hell are you guys doing? This is my car."
"This car belongs to the bank.
It's being repossessed."
One of the men presented Janai with some papers.
Not to be outdone, Janai turned on her charm.
"Look, as you can see, I'm pregnant and I just need to go to the hospital for a moment. I'm having complications with my pregnancy. Just let me go and I promise to bring the car back."

The tow men looked at each other and laughed.
"Nice try lady, but we have orders to bring this back in."
"Well, what if I gave you a few dollars would you be able to leave it here with me then?"
"Nothing we can do, lady. Even if you had the full amount, once we come out here we don't accept any form of payment, we just come to collect the goods."

Janai was fuming by this time. "Well, fuck you then!" She stomped off back into her apartment. Janai was frustrated. She hadn't felt this helpless since she was a little girl watching her daddy beat her mother. She sat on the couch and cried uncontrollably.

After thirty minutes, Janai pulled herself together and gathered up the courage to call Chanel and ask for help. Chanel's voicemail indicated that she was out of town.

"What? Where in the hell can she be?"

Her ego wouldn't let her call Jordan. As a last resort she called Micki. Through tears, Janai explained her situation to Micki. Micki listened without passing judgment. She told Janai that she could stay with her until she got her life back on track.

Janai was packed and ready when Micki arrived an hour later.

"Thanks Micki, I really appreciate this." Janai gave Micki a heartfelt hug and the two ladies left for Micki's place.

Micki showed Janai to her upstairs bedroom. The room was large, but plain. It had not yet been decorated. There were no pictures on the wall or any other kind of adornments.

A twin-sized bed with a dresser and a nightstand were all the pieces of furniture in there. A phone sat on the nightstand. There were also some boxes filled with junk in the corner.

"You can use this room, Janai. I want you to feel completely comfortable here, so you don't have to ask to eat, wash clothes, or whatever the case may be. When you need something just go use it. This is your home now."

Janai nodded. Micki also showed Janai where to find the linens and toiletries.

"Alright, just holler if you need anything." Micki left Janai to freshen up.

When Janai was done soaking she came downstairs and saw Micki reading a book and drinking some cocoa. It was unusually cold for October in Atlanta. Micki looked up at Janai and noticed a sullen look in her eyes. She put her book down. "What's wrong Janai? You look troubled."

Janai had a sarcastic tone in her voice as she twisted her mouth to speak.

"Of course, I look troubled. I'm pregnant with no home and no money. I'm totally dependent on another person."

"Sit down, Janai." Janai sat in the recliner adjacent from Micki. "Look, instead of you stressing yourself, why don't you just concentrate on having a healthy pregnancy. You know what you have to do to survive. Once you have a baby, just go full speed ahead."

"I now, it's just hard to start over, and that's basically what I'm doing." Janai said fighting back tears.

"How did all of this get started? I mean, with your situation, how did things get to this point?"

Janai was hesitant to tell Micki the real deal. Even though she was helping her out, Janai still felt as though she was too judgmental. But Micki did at least deserve the truth. Janai bit her lip. She fessed up to everything; from the affair to getting fired to squandering money and to Jordan leaving, after he learned the truth. She also told her that she felt as if she were above getting financial aid and food stamps.

"Excuse me? I don't know who spoiled you, but you better learn how to swallow your pride when you need help."
"How am I spoiled?"
Micki rolled her eyes. "Girl, please. Are you kidding me? Look in your suitcase. All of your clothes are name brands. Your purses are Prada and Gucci, and even your perfumes are by Ralph Lauren and Calvin Klein. And you had a really expensive car for the type of salary you were making."

Janai got really defensive and started waving her hands around. "So? What's wrong with that? I mean, I see you living high on the hog. I mean everything up in here is plush."
"True Janai, but I didn't always have it like this. I sacrificed and saved. Look Janai, I'm not trying to

176

belittle you." Micki walked over and took Janai's hand.

"The next time around, you need to live the lifestyle that you can afford. You have a lot of nice things but nothing to show for it. If I was getting money from a man, I'd be banking it. You gotta think smart, Janai. If you use a man, at least use him to your advantage. Think long term. You should want longevity, especially now with a child on the way."

Janai listened to Micki's advice and hoped that she would get a second chance.

Chanel's business trip to San Francisco left her feeling a little jet lagged. When she got home she didn't even unpack, she just threw her roll-a-way bag in the corner of her bedroom.

She undressed and left the clothes in the middle of the floor and put on her thick bathrobe. Then she listened to her messages. She was disappointed that she hadn't received a message from Janai. She had tried to call her several times before she left town. She didn't like the way things last ended. She simply wanted to help her friend.

Chanel took a long, hot shower. Afterwards, she grabbed a pillow and a blanket and took it to the couch in the living room to take a nap. As soon as Chanel's head hit the pillow, there was a knock on her door. "Damn! Who the hell is this?" she said aloud to herself. "Can't even close my eyes for a minute."

Chanel looked through her peephole and couldn't believe her eyes. It was Donnell. "Ain't this a bitch!" She snatched her door open.

"I see I've gotta change my gate code. Donnell, what the hell are you doing here?"

"I had to see you."

"Why?"

"I've been trying to reach you, but you haven't returned any of my phone calls."

"So, you just took it upon yourself to pop up at my place, huh?"

"You left me no choice, especially since you hung up on me when I was spilling my heart to you."

"Donnell, look I'm tired. I just got in from a business trip and all I want to do is take a nap. So, if you don't mind." Chanel tried to close the door, but Donnell wouldn't let her.

"Chanel, just wait. Just give me a few minutes to talk to you. Just hear me and I'll leave."

Chanel relented. "Fine!"

"May I come in?"

"No, whatever you have to say, you can say it right here." Chanel didn't trust herself being along with him.

"Okay, well I just want to say that I love you, Chanel. I mean, I really love you and I didn't realize it until after you were gone."

Chanel rolled her eyes. "Right. *You* love *me*?"

"Yes, why is that so hard to believe?" Donnell was puzzled.

"You really have to ask that after your track record…the man full of false promises and lies."

"Chanel I want you back in my life. I need you in my life. You are an incredible woman and I'd be a fool to just let you go. I plan on fighting for your love. It's worth fighting for. I want us to be together again, Chanel."

"Why? So you can just string me along for another five years?"

"No, you don't understand. I want to share everything with you. I want a partner for life."

He took his hands to her face as if to stroke it. He reached inside the pocket of his leather jacket and pulled out a single but beautiful, flawless, marquis-cut diamond engagement ring. Donnell took Chanel's hand in his.

"Chanel Jackson, I want you to marry me. Will you be my wife, my friend, my confidant, my life partner?"

Chanel gasped for air. Tears had begun to run down her face. She had waited five years for this moment and now that it was here, she was speechless. She hadn't seen this coming. This was the Donnell of her dreams. He was tender, vulnerable and sweet. He kissed her softly on the lips and put the ring on her third finger.

"Look, I know you love me and you still want to be with me. I can feel it. But I won't pressure you. Just wear this for a few days and I'll be back for my answer."

Donnell kissed Chanel on the lips and walked away leaving her standing in the doorway, dazed and confused.

Chapter 22

For the first time that Donnell could remember, he was sincere in his words and with his actions. He was not running game on Chanel. He really *did* want to marry her. He hoped she felt the same way, too.

His mind was spinning. Donnell wished he could talk to his mother. He really needed her right now. He called the next best thing… his Pops. Donnell's father had always been a great friend whom Donnell could always count on in times of need. He called his father as soon as he got home. He was feeling rather anxious.

After beating around the bush and making small talk, Donnell's father cut to the chase.
"Now, tell me Donnell, what's the real reason you called? Tell me what's on your mind, son?"
Donnell laughed. Both of his parents could always tell when something was weighing on him.
"I've asked Chanel to marry me."
"Well, I think it's about time, don't you? What's the problem?"
"I messed up. I messed up real bad and I'm not sure if she still wants me. But I love her with all my heart."
"Then, the only thing you can do is work your ass off to get her to accept your proposal." His Pops was old, but he was still sharp and witty.

"You need to pull out all the stops, with reason of course. You see son, you don't want to make a fool of yourself in the process. A woman won't respect you then. Just know when to bow out gracefully. Now I can't tell you what to do, but let me give you a piece of advice. Dig deep into her soul. Make her feel special, like she's the only woman that exists. Pay attention to her wants and needs. The things that she's done for you are probably the same kinds of things she wants done for her. Now go on and get your woman."

Donnell and his father shared a laugh. "Okay, Dad, I love you."

"I love you, too, son."

****

Chanel couldn't sleep. All she could do was stare at the ring Donnell had given her. She felt as if Donnell was being genuine, but there were other times in the past when she felt like he was being genuine and it was nothing more than lies.

"What do I do?" she asked out loud. "I love him, but I can't trust him. What kind of marriage can I possibly have without trust?"

She had all types of thoughts racing through her mind. She decided to give her mother a call before going to bed. Chanel told her mother what her dilemma was.

Her mother told her the decision shouldn't be that hard. If you have to ask the question, then perhaps you already know the answer. She told her that there was more to a marriage than just love.

"There's loyalty, commitment, and above all trust. Is what he's bringing to the table enough for you? Only you can answer these questions. Trust your heart."

"You sure aren't making it easy for me, momma." Chanel was distressed.

"I'm not going to tell you what you want to hear, Chanel. I'm always going to tell you what you need to know. Anyway, I'm off my soapbox."

She pleaded with her mother not to say anything to the rest of the family, especially her Aunt Cicely.

"Alright baby, you take care. I love you."

"I love you, too, momma."

Although Chanel was tired, thoughts of Donnell and what their life could be like kept her lying awake for another hour. Eventually she drifted off into a happy and peaceful sleep.

The next morning Chanel almost overslept. She jumped up out of bed and went straight for the shower. After her shower she noticed the time. She couldn't be late today, for she had an important briefing to attend.

She grabbed something simple to wear. A magenta sweater and a pair of black slacks with some knee high boots. She quickly splashed some perfume on her neck and wrists. She always liked to smell good. Her hair was wrapped up in a scarf so all she had to do was comb it down and be on her merry way.

Chanel grabbed her coat, hat and purse and headed for work. Normally she did the speed limit, but this day she had a heavy foot. She didn't want to be late. She got to work right on time. When Chanel arrived, she immediately checked her e-mail. She was surprised to see that Donnell had sent her one. Chanel noticed the time it was sent. This made her smile. She took a look at the ring he gave her then double clicked on the e-mail.

His e-mail was short and sweet. *Just wanted to let you know that I was thinking about you...I love you.*

She smiled again. She decided not to respond to his e-mail for the moment. She just saved it. One of her co-workers had made a fresh pot of coffee. Chanel poured herself a cup. She needed all the pep she could get. Once Chanel got caught up on her work she had a little free time and decided to give Janai a call. All she got was an answering machine. *Why isn't she taking my calls*, Chanel wondered. Chanel dialed Micki's number next, but before she could finish, someone knocked on her office door.

A delivery person had come with a bouquet of roses in a pretty glass vase.

Chanel took the clipboard and signed her name. Her co-workers were staring at her. She took the roses to her nose to rub it on their faces as they looked on. There were red, white and pink roses all mixed together. The card attached read: *the white one's are for how much I value our friendship, the red one's are for our undying love for one another and the pink one's are for how bright our future can be together. Love, Donnell.*

Chanel was moved by Donnell's romantic gesture. A nosey co-worker poked her head in the office to see what was up. "Well, well, well, what have we here?"

"Just some flowers, that's all." Chanel didn't like people in her business, especially at work. She was a private person.

"Humph! Wonder what you had to do to get those?" "Don't even worry about it, Sheila." Chanel was about to rip into her, but her phone rang. She quickly answered it. It was Micki. She was calling to find out why Chanel hadn't told her about Donnell's proposal.

"I knew that mother of mine couldn't hold water," Chanel laughed.

After spending majority of the time on the phone talking about Donnell and what he had been up to, Chanel asked Micki if she had heard from Janai. She told her how she had been trying to reach her to no avail.

"You can speak to her now if you want. She's staying here with me temporarily."
"What? Why?" Chanel was bewildered.
"Long story, but I'll let her tell you."
"Well, why don't we all just meet for lunch at about one o'clock?

Micki and Janai met Chanel at her office. They ooh-ed and aah-ed over Chanel's ring and flowers. Janai took a closer look at Chanel's ring. "Damn girl, this shit looks like the Hope Diamond."
"Janai, you are so dramatic, it's not *that* big."
"No, I'm serious, Chanel. I gotta give it to Donnell. I mean we all know I'm no fan of his, but he must really want to be with you 'cause that shit on your finger ain't cheap. So what you gon' do cow?"
"I don't know yet." Chanel went to quickly check her e-mails before they headed out. Just as she was about to sign out she received another e-mail. It was from Donnell's cell phone. All it said was for her to come to the parking lot and to look up.

The women made it outside. Micki and Janai were just as anxious to find out what else Donnell had in store for Chanel.

When Chanel looked up she could hardly believe her eyes. There was a small airplane circling the building with a banner that read, MARRY ME CHANEL! I LOVE YOU!

"Oh, my God!" Chanel shouted. She was in awe.
All the commotion caused her co-workers to run outside to see what was going on. They all clapped when they saw the airplane with the banner tied to it. There were all types of comments coming from the sidelines. Men were shouting. Women were cheering. *"If you don't marry him, I will."*
"Girl, her man is fine, she better marry him!"
"Don't be no fool!"

Chanel just stood there with her hands covering her mouth. "I can't believe this. I just cannot believe this."

Chapter 23

Janai's back was aching. Every time she tried to sit down and relax, she had to get up and go to the bathroom. She was also famished. She went downstairs to raid the refrigerator.

She pushed herself all the way to the foot of the bed with her arms until her legs slid off the bed, then, she was able to ease off the bed. It had become a major task for her to do simple things that are normally taken for granted. When she finally got on her feet she took a deep breath as if she had just finished running the last mile in a marathon. Janai stopped at the mirror before going downstairs. She stared at herself. She became depressed by her appearance. She thought she looked fat and dumpy. Her nose had spread and her face was fat. Nevertheless, that didn't stop her from stuffing her face.

Janai ate the steak and baked potato she had leftover from lunch. After she finished her meal, Janai plopped down on the sofa in the living room to watch TV. She just couldn't manage the struggle up the stairs to her room. She was flipping through the channels when the phone rang. She figured Micki must have picked it up because it didn't ring for that long. Micki called out to Janai to pick up. It was Chanel calling for her. She wanted to know what was really going on with Janai. She had decided at lunch she wouldn't bring it up. She just wanted them to have a good time and Chanel would wait until she could speak with Janai in private.

Janai filled her in on everything. "I just wish all of this were over, Chanel."
"Janai, I know you don't really want this child...why not?"
"I don't want to end up like my fucked up parents. I want the baby to be in a loving, safe environment with someone who will love and care for him or her. I'm just not capable of doing it right now or ever."
"You almost sound like you want to give the child up for adoption."
"Jordan wouldn't go for that, if it's his. If it is, I'll just let him raise the child and I'll go on about my business. It all boils down to me not wanting to be a mother right now... maybe in a few years or so, but not right now."

They both got quiet for a moment, each lost in their own thoughts.
Before hanging up, Chanel reassured her best friend that she would be there for her, regardless of her decision.

After they hung up, Janai propped up her feet and fell asleep watching Oprah.

Chanel had put in long hours at the station, and she was still feeling overwhelmed by all that happened to Janai. She relaxed in her Jacuzzi thinking about how she could help her.

She hadn't spoken to Donnell since he proposed. She looked down at her left hand and smiled. Even in the darkness, the ring on her finger shined so bright. It glistened like the stars in the sky.

Chanel gave Donnell a call. After all, she did at least want to let him know what she thought of his surprises. She leaned out of her Jacuzzi and reached for the cordless phone that she had placed in a patio chair near her. Chanel felt like a nervous sixteen-year-old girl, who was calling a boy for the very first time. After the fourth ring, Donnell answered the phone just as Chanel was about to disconnect. He sounded out of breath, as if he'd been running.

"Are you busy?" Chanel's voice was high.
"No, no, I just got out of the shower that's all. I heard the phone and I snatched a towel and ran across the hall."
She smirked, taking pleasure in the thought that only a small towel was covering his wet, smooth, chocolate body.

Donnell didn't think that he'd be hearing so soon from Chanel. He hoped that meant she had an answer for him, and hopefully the right answer. He was somewhat disappointed when she said she was just calling to thank him for the roses and the airplane. He wanted to hear her say that she would be his wife.

But even so, Donnell beamed. He was glad he could bring a smile to her face and make her happy even if it was only for a brief moment.

While they were in the moment, he tried to sell her on the idea of marriage. He told her that they'd have an incredible future together and that he'd spend the rest of his life making her happy. With that, he tried to worm his way over to her house.

"Why don't you let me come on over there tonight and keep you warm?"

"No, I don't think that would be a good idea."

"Why not?"

She didn't want their lovemaking to suggest anything. Chanel also knew that she was still in love with Donnell, therefore she was extremely vulnerable. She needed to continue to be strong.

"Chanel, I just want to be next to you that's all. I want to feel your soft skin next to mine and smell you. You always smell so good and…"

She was getting hotter by the minute listening to him talk. "Look Donnell, I'm not trying to be rude but I don't want this right now, okay?"

"Ok, ok, I can respect that. But at least let me take you to breakfast tomorrow, or we can meet for brunch."

"No, the truth is I just need some time away from you. I need time to sort out my feelings and figure out what it is that I want and if that includes you in my future."

There was immediate silence. Donnell's tone changed.

"Alright then, I understand. And I'll be around if you change your mind." Chanel could hear the hurt in his voice.

Donnell's expertise in the bed had always been Chanel's downfall. She refused to be swayed by some dick, even if it was some *damn good dick*! She got out of the Jacuzzi and took a cold shower.

Chapter 24

On Sunday morning Janai was up earlier than usual. She felt very uncomfortable. The baby was kicking her hard in her rib cage and her abdomen felt like it was tightening up.

Three hours after Janai woke up, she heard Micki's alarm clock chime. Janai wobbled downstairs and loaded the dishwasher. Then she put on some water to boil tea while she fixed herself an omelet with cheese, bell peppers, onions, and bacon and a slice of toast. Micki came into the kitchen about an hour later.

"Smells good down here, what are you eating?"
"Just eggs and toast." Janai answered between bites.
"Yeah right, it looks like you could feed an army."
Janai smiled. "Hey I need all the nutrients I can get. After all I am eating for two now." She patted her belly.
"Yeah well, I'm about to leave in a few minutes to pick up some folks and head to church. You're welcome to come if you like," Micki offered.

The thought of going to church made Janai cringe. She hadn't stepped a foot inside a church since she was about seven or eight years old when her grandmother used to take her. She imagined the church would immediately start burning if she walked in with all the sins she'd committed.

"No thanks. I'll just stay here."

"You sure?"

Janai nodded.

"Well the invitation still stands anytime you want to go."

"Thanks, but no. Maybe another time."

When Janai finished eating breakfast, she put those dishes in the dishwasher and let it run. She decided to call Jordan, she hadn't spoken to him since the fallout. She was sort of edgy, but she needed to call him to let him know what was going on with her. Besides that, she needed him to take her to her ob-gyn appointment. She reached him on his cell.

Jordan was surprised that she hadn't landed on her feet this time. "So you couldn't find another sucker to give you any money huh?" Although Jordan didn't take pleasure in anyone's misery, not even Janai's, he couldn't help messing with her just a little. Deep down inside he was still really hurt by the whole situation. Once he agreed to pick her up, he rushed her off the phone. He didn't feel like re-hashing all of the past drama.

Tuesday morning came and Jordan showed up promptly. Janai came to the door with her purse and was ready to go. They were both pretty cordial to one another.

"Hey, J!"

"Hi Janai." They both felt ill at ease.

Janai noticed a frown on Jordan's face. She had seen that same look of disgust many times. *He probably thinks I'm fat as hell*, she thought.

But Jordan was his normal sweet self. He didn't say anything about her weight. Jordan opened the door for Janai and helped her get up in his pick up truck. He went around to the driver's side, hopped in and they were headed to the doctor's office.

They sat in uncomfortable silence for about two blocks until Jordan broke the quietness. "You said your doctor's office is downtown, right?"

Janai nodded. "On Peachtree." Janai wanted to keep the conversation going. "I'm pretty big, huh?" Jordan smiled and looked at Janai, then at her belly. "You just picked up a few pounds, but that's to be expected. You look good. Besides, after you give birth, I'm sure you'll be back to your normal size in no time."

Janai looked at him in disbelief.

"I'm serious, Janai. You're one of the few women I've seen who *really* looks beautiful pregnant. Pregnancy agrees with you."

Although Jordan despised Janai's ways, he still loved her. He found it hard to stay mad at her. He wanted to have a normal conversation without arguing.

"Now I know you're blowing smoke up my ass. But it's cool, because I know you're just being sweet."

Then the conversation took a turn for the worse. Jordan had pissed Janai off. He started asking her if she had found a job yet. And once the baby is born, how does she plan on making ends meet and what about transportation and so on.

"Look J, you're beginning to piss me off with all these stupid ass questions."
Jordan ignored her and continued to drive. Janai shook her head and looked out the passenger's side window. The two didn't speak for the remainder of the ride.

Once they arrived, Jordan sat with Janai in the waiting area. When the nurse called Janai's name, Jordan got up, too.
Janai rolled her eyes at Jordan. "Is *your* name Janai Love?" Her tone was very unwelcoming.

"Look Janai, I would like to go into the exam room with you, if you don't mind. I want to see what goes on."
Although she'd never admit to it, Janai wanted Jordan to go with her as a means of support. She shrugged her shoulders. "I don't care. You can come if you want."

They followed the nurse to the back where Janai's vitals were taken.

Janai disrobed and put on the examination gown that the nurse gave her. She and Jordan waited in uncomfortable silence for the doctor.

After a short while, Dr. Thompson entered the room. She didn't see Jordan sitting in the corner until she closed the door. "I see we have a visitor today, huh?"

Janai nodded. The doctor shook Jordan's hand. "I'm Dr. Thompson, nice to meet you."

Dr. Thompson wondered if Jordan was the baby's father, but Janai did not offer that information and Dr. Thompson didn't ask.

"Let's get started." Dr. Thompson washed her hands and put on some latex gloves.

Dr. Thompson besieged Janai with questions as she was examining her. "How has your appetite been? Have you been smoking? Drinking? Riding motorcycles?"

Janai chuckled. "Fine. No. No and definitely not!" She had been drinking some alcoholic beverages from time to time, but not enough that she felt was worth mentioning. Besides, Jordan would blow his top. He already thought that Janai drank too much anyway.

The doctor pressed on Janai's abdomen a few times. The baby replied by giving a strong kick. This made Janai wince in slight discomfort.

"He's kicking?" Jordan asked, assuming it was a boy.

"Yes, place your hands right here, I'm sure he or she will kick again." Jordan hopped up from his chair and laid his hand on Janai's belly.

"Wow. I've never felt anything like this." He continued to feel the baby move around and without thinking he laid his head on her belly. Jordan could hear some sloshing sounds.

Janai stared at Jordan. She had a soft, tender smile on her face. Jordan returned the smile. *Damn I hope this child is mine*, he thought to himself.

The doctor interrupted this warm moment. "Would you like to find out the baby's sex?"

Before Janai could answer Jordan said yes. Janai didn't care about the sex of the baby. She wanted to remain as detached as possible. The doctor looked at Janai for approval. Janai shrugged her shoulders and nodded yes.

Dr. Thompson rubbed some jelly on Janai's stomach and they all looked at the ultra sound monitor. She pointed out the baby's head, legs, and feet. Within a few minutes she was able to make out the sex. "Congratulations! It's a girl!"

Jordan was ecstatic. Janai was unaffected by the news.

When they left the doctor's office, Janai asked Jordan to stop by the grocery store on the way home so she could pick up some fruit. He stopped by a store that was near Micki's place. Jordan remained in the car listening to the radio.

Janai purchased four items: two limes, one apple and some frozen margarita mix. She paid for her items and had the cashier place them in a brown paper bag so Jordan could not see what was inside. She walked back to the car eating her apple.

"I guess you really were craving for fruit, huh," Jordan asked as he helped her get back in his pick-up.

"More than you know," she replied, still munching on the apple.

Janai headed straight for the kitchen after Jordan dropped her off at home. She placed her bag on the counter and reached in the top cabinet for the blender. Janai's abdomen tightened. She squinted her eyes and grabbed her stomach in agony. She made it to the couch and laid there for a while. Janai was still on the sofa when Micki came home.

"Hey Janai, are you ok," Micki asked when she saw Janai lounging on the couch.

"I think so. I just felt a little dizzy and my stomach sort of tightened up on me."

"Did you call your doctor?"

"No, I just came from there. But it's okay. I felt like this yesterday and I was okay. Once I relaxed for a little while, I was fine."

"Alright now. Don't be up in here having me delivering no babies." They both laughed.

"I won't. I'm fine."

Micki walked off into the kitchen as the phone was ringing. "Janai, can you get that?" she yelled. It was Jordan. He was calling to let Janai know that her wallet had fallen out of her purse and he would bring it by later that evening.

Micki came out of the kitchen holding the margarita mix.

"You wanna explain this, Janai?"

"Oh I was planning on just having a small drink." She tried to sugar coat the fact that she was drinking at all.

Micki told her that she wouldn't stand for it. Not under her roof. If she was going to drink, she'd have to leave. Micki was not going to be responsible for the retardation or death of a child.

"Fine Micki, I'll take the shit back." Janai snatched it from Micki and wobbled upstairs.

An hour later she heard Micki knocking on her bedroom door. "What," Janai said dryly.

Micki told her she was going to pick up some Chinese food and wanted to know if she wanted anything. Janai wanted nothing, but a drink.

When she heard the door close, she went downstairs to see if she had really driven off. Then, she hurried down to the kitchen and made a margarita with the unopened bottle of Tequila that Micki brought back from Cancun.

Janai took a long sip and savored the flavor. Then she took her drink upstairs just in case Micki showed up.
"Who the hell does she think she is? Shit, I'm a grown-ass woman. I can do what I please." Janai always talked to herself when she drank.

A few minutes later the phone rang. It was Jordan telling Janai that he was on his way over with her wallet.
Damn, she thought. *Why now?* She guzzled down the rest of her drink and went upstairs to brush her teeth so that Jordan wouldn't smell liquor on her breath.

Janai heard the doorbell ding. She started down the stairs to answer the door. She lost her footing on the second step. The combination of drinking and the weight of a very swollen belly caused Janai to tumble down the stairs. She did not move. Janai was unconscious.

Jordan knocked and knocked and rang the bell several times, but no answer. He even used his cell phone to call. *Maybe she was in the bathroom, or maybe in another part of the house where she was unable to hear the doorbell,* he thought After several attempts he was worried and tried to look through the windows but the blinds were closed. Jordan walked around to the back of the house to see if he saw Janai, but those blinds were closed as well. When he went back to the front of the house, he saw Micki pull into the driveway. She got out of her car carrying bags of Chinese food.

"Hi Jordan, what are you doing here?"
"Hey Micki, I came by to bring Janai her wallet. I just spoke with her a few minutes ago, but she's not answering the door."
"Well, come on in. I'll go upstairs and see if she's sleep or something." Micki opened the door and saw Janai sprawled out at the bottom of the stairs. She covered her mouth and gasped.
"Oh my God!" Micki dropped her food and went to feel for Janai's pulse.
"She's still breathing, Jordan."
"Oh my God," he kept repeating as he called 911.

The technicians arrived ten minutes later. They asked a few important questions and put Janai in the back of the ambulance. Jordan rode with them. Micki got in her car and sped to the hospital.

Janai was taken to the prenatal unit so that both she and her baby could be monitored. Jordan gave Janai's information to the admissions associate. He paced the floor while he waited on some news about Janai's condition. Micki paced, too. Less than ten minutes later, the on-call physician came out to update Jordan and Micki. Before the doctor could say a word, Jordan was already interrogating the man.

"What's going on? Is she going to be ok? And what about the baby?"
"Sir, please calm down. We're doing everything we can to stabilize her and the baby."
What does that mean?" Jordan had a nervous look on his face. Micki tried to be calm, but she was nervous, too.
The physician explained that Janai's blood pressure was unusually high. There was a risk to the unborn child and they were going to have to induce labor and deliver by c-section. The doctor explained that even at thirty weeks there's a slight risk involved with premature births. He also went on to say that they found high alcohol content in Janai's blood. He was afraid that the baby could have fetal alcohol syndrome.

"What?" Alcohol?" Jordan bit down on his lip and gritted his teeth. He was furious! Micki just shook her head in bewilderment. They had to operate right away. The doctor left Jordan with his anger.

Jordan continued to pace the floor. He was livid! He punched his right fist into his hand. "How in the hell could she be so irresponsible? Alcohol? My child better live. If my daughter dies because of her stupid ass, I will never forgive her." Jordan had already begun to feel as if the child were his. Micki smiled and gave him a hug. She could tell that he really cared about the baby. She also told him about how she drank in Vegas and about the incident in her kitchen.

The physician came back about a half hour later, this time with a smile on his face. The baby had been born seven minutes ago. She was tiny, but she would be ok. Janai was in recovery. The drugs would wear off shortly. The baby was in Neonatal Intensive Care Unit. She only weighed two pounds at birth. Micki and Jordan were told that the baby's breathing and temperature needed to be monitored and they also needed to make sure her lungs were fully developed.

Jordan wanted to see her right away. The nurse gave Jordan a set of yellow scrubs. He had to wear them because premature babies are extremely susceptible to germs, and they can get sick very easily.

The nurse showed him a very tiny, caramel-colored baby. Jordan instantly fell in love. Tears flowed down his face like a waterfall. He wasn't allowed to pick her up just yet, because she was hooked up to so many tubes. He studied the baby real hard. He couldn't tell who she looked like because her face was scrunched up and she was asleep. He reached inside the incubator and touched her miniature-sized fingers.

He saw that the baby's cuticles were dark and so were her earlobes. *She's mine.* He said a little prayer and thanked God for his beautiful daughter.

Chapter 25

Chanel had gone to a local sports bar with Tony Velez. Over the last few weeks, they had become great friends. They were half way into their conversation when Tony noticed a sparkling ring on her third finger.

"Wait a minute. What is this?"
Chanel was not materialistic, but she absolutely loved the ring. She wore it everywhere, even though she had not given Donnell an answer yet.

"Oh, it's an engagement ring," she said coolly.
"Ok, let me rephrase the question. What's up with that?"
She smiled. "Donnell asked me to marry him."
"So, why are you out with me?"
Chanel gave him the old "friends" speech. Tony was disappointed. After all, he had been trying to get next to Chanel for quite some time, and every time he got close to her something always happened. And that something was Donnell.

"The only thing I have to say is if you do accept his proposal, I hope he treats you right. He's one lucky man, that's for damn sure. And if you ever need me for anything, I want you to call me. We can always be friends, Chanel, whether you're married or not. Ok?"

"Okay." Chanel's cell phone rang while they were still talking, it was Micki.

"Excuse me, Tony." She answered her phone. "What's up cousin?"

Chanel abruptly hung up the phone and jumped up from her seat. Tony frowned wondering what was going on with her.

"What's wrong?"

Chanel struggled to put her coat on and grab her purse. She was upset.

"My best friend is in the hospital."

"Do you need me to drive?"

"No." Chanel ran to her car.

Chanel had to drive across town from the sports bar to get to the hospital. There was an accident on the freeway so traffic was backed up and it took her an hour before she arrived.

Micki had given her the room number over the phone. Chanel entered Janai's room and gasped at her friend who looked lifeless. Chanel turned to Micki who was sitting in a chair opposite Jordan.

"What happened?"

"Janai fell down the stairs. We found her and had her rushed here."

Chanel looked at Micki as if she couldn't believe what she was saying and then looked back at Janai. This time, noticing that her stomach wasn't as big as it had been lately. She put her hands over her mouth again.

"Oh, my God! The baby! Is it…"

Jordan cut her off midstream. "No Chanel, the baby is fine. They had to take her early because Janai was in such distress."

"Her?" Chanel smiled.

"Yes. I have a daughter," he smiled. And she's the most beautiful creature you'll ever lay eyes on."

"I would like to see her. Where is she?"

Jordan got up from out of his chair. "Come on, I'll take you."

Micki waited in the room while Jordan and Chanel went to see the baby.

Jordan filled Chanel in, on as much of the details that he could. After Chanel saw the baby, they went back downstairs to check on Janai.

"Any change," Jordan asked Micki.

"No. Nothing."

"I can't believe she jeopardized my child's life."

Jordan started going off and saying how selfish Janai is and that he wasn't worried about Janai, just his daughter. Chanel couldn't believe what he was saying. She was taken aback by his coldness.

A few minutes later the physician came in to check Janai's vitals. As he did, her body started going into convulsions. Jordan, Micki and Chanel all hopped up out of their chairs and gathered around to see what was going on. The doctor called for assistance and ordered them all out of the room.

Chanel was visibly upset. She went outside to get some air. She sat outside for a moment, then, it began to get cold, so she headed back into the hospital. Before she could make it back in, her cell phone rang. It was Donnell.

"Hey babe, what's up?"

"I'm at the hospital. Janai delivered the baby prematurely."

"I'm coming up there to be with you. What unit is Janai in?"

She filled him in on the location. When he arrived, Donnell embraced Chanel.

"You alright?"

She shrugged her shoulders. "I'm just waiting for them to come out of that room and tell us something."

"Come on, sit down." She and Donnell sat down. Micki and Jordan had come from the cafeteria.

"Thought you might need this," Micki handed Chanel a cup of hot coffee.

"Thanks." They all sat quietly, each praying for Janai.

Without any indication, Tony also appeared at the hospital to offer comfort to Chanel. He said he wanted to check on her and see how Janai was doing. Chanel gave him a few pertinent details but let him know that she wasn't out of danger, yet.

Donnell looked at him crazy and they got into it for a minute. Donnell told him that his presence was not needed, and motioned his hand as if he were shooing a fly.

"Why don't you just let Chanel decide that *partner*," Tony turned to Chanel for a reply.

"Hey! Both of you stop it!" Chanel was upset enough as it was. This little show only made her more distressed.

"Tony, I'm fine for now. If I need you, I'll call you okay?"

"Yeah." He left as quickly as he had come.

The doctor came out as soon as Tony left. "Ms. Love is fine. She just had an allergic reaction to the medication we administered earlier. You all can come back in the room now if you want."

They all marched back into the room to find Janai moving and trying to focus her eyes. She was a bit groggy. She saw the four of them standing over her.

"What the hell y'all lookin' at?"

They all laughed. "Well, she's alright," Chanel said. Immediately Janai wanted to know what was going on and why she was there. Once they all filled her in, Janai touched her stomach and panicked. Even though Janai wasn't ready to be a mother, she didn't want the baby to die.

Jordan was still so infuriated with Janai he went off on her. He let her have it. He wondered why she was so concerned now about the baby. She should've been concerned during the earlier trimesters when she was drinking. She wasn't concerned then. He could've choked her, right then and there.

"Is she pretty?" Janai asked Chanel meekly.

"Just beautiful," Chanel beamed.

"I want to see her." Janai tried to push herself up from the bed, but felt lightheaded.

Both Jordan and Micki told her she needed to wait for clearance from a doctor to move about. Even though she was coherent, she was still heavily sedated.

"I'm glad you're okay, Janai," Donnell told her. "Chanel, I'll be out in the waiting area."

Chanel nodded. She sat and talked with her friend for a little while and then decided she was exhausted. She told Janai she was going to get some rest and would be back in the morning. Meanwhile, Donnell was still in the waiting area. His eyes were growing heavy. He was exhausted, too.

Chanel tapped him on the shoulder. Donnell jumped. She told him she was tired and would be back in the morning. He looked at his watch and realized it was after one o'clock in the morning. He was exhausted and didn't want to drive that far. He asked Chanel if he could use her spare bedroom for the night. Chanel cringed.

"I promise, no funny stuff, Chanel. I respect you too much. I just don't want to fall asleep at the wheel on my way home."

Chanel agreed and they both rode in her car. When they got to her place Donnell went straight to the spare bedroom. He turned on the light and closed the door only partially. Chanel's room was diagonally across from the spare room; she could see Donnell in her mirror. Chanel watched Donnell get undressed. First his shirt and then his pants and boxer shorts. Donnell always slept in the nude. The idea of his naked chocolate body made Chanel wet between the legs.

When Donnell went to turn out the light, Chanel stepped back a little so he wouldn't see her staring. She closed her door, undressed and hopped in the shower. She let the water gently caress her breasts wishing it were Donnell's lips. She touched herself between her legs and imagined it was Donnell moving inside her. It had been a while since she made love and she wanted Donnell in a bad way. She finished her shower and dried off. She reached in her middle drawer and put on a very sheer teddy then, went across the hall to where Donnell was sleeping.

She opened her bedroom door and went into the spare bedroom. She quietly called out to Donnell. No response. *Maybe he was already asleep*, she thought.
Chanel moved closer to the bed, she felt the covers, but Donnell wasn't in bed. Then she walked toward

the living room and noticed that the refrigerator door was ajar.

Donnell was looking for something in the fridge and hadn't noticed Chanel walking up to him.

"Donnell, what are you doing?" Her heart skipped when she saw his over-sized dick hanging free between his legs.

"Oh, I was thirsty." He raised his eyebrows wondering what was going on. The lights were off but the light from the fridge was enough for him to get an eyeful of Chanel standing in a sheer black teddy. He could see her silhouette. He could also see that her nipples through the sheer material were hard and calling out for him to come and get a taste.

Chanel walked up to him and kissed him deeply. " I want you tonight. I need you tonight." Chanel was stroking Donnell, making him rock hard. Then she grabbed his hand and placed it under her teddy. Donnell could feel the love juices on his fingers. In one fluid move, Donnell sat Chanel on the kitchen counter. They tore into each other like savage beasts in heat. There was licking, sucking, sticking and rolling. After everything was said and done they had both worn each other out. Chanel fell asleep in Donnell's arms.

Donnell was wide awake. He had never before felt passion from Chanel until tonight. He could tell from their love making that her answer to his marriage proposal would be yes. He drifted off to sleep, dreaming of Chanel and the life they were going to have together.

Chapter 26

Janai was light-headed and sore but she demanded to see her child. The nurses weren't allowed to bring the baby to Janai since she was hooked up to monitors, but her mother could come to her.

Janai continued to argue with the nurse as only Janai could. Jordan sat in a chair next to her.
"Look damn it! I am her mother and *I'll* tell you what's going to happen with my own child. Do you hear me?"

The quiet, blonde nurse was fresh out of nursing school; Janai's outbursts left the young nurse shaken. The nurse told her once her medication wore off, when she was less woozy; they would allow her to go up to the nursery area to see her baby. Janai continued to raise hell. Jordan decided to intervene. He knew Janai wouldn't stop until she got her way.
"Why don't I take her up in a wheelchair? I'll keep a close eye on her."
Hesitantly, the nurse agreed. After she went to get the chair she sat it as close to the bed as possible and she and Jordan helped Janai into it.

Jordan wheeled Janai to the nursery and when they tried to enter, they found the door locked. The hospital made sure no one but staff and parents had admittance to that area. An older nurse checked

Janai and Jordan's wristbands. Jordan wheeled her up to a baby box that read 'Baby Love' on it. They had not yet named her.

When Janai laid eyes on her daughter she just smiled. It was as if she were at peace with everything. "Is this my baby?"
There were no chairs in the nursery, so Jordan stood against the wall near the two of them.
"That's her," he said in the softest voice ever.
Janai took her forefinger and rubbed it against the baby's soft chin.
"Look at her; she's beautiful just like you said. She's so pretty and brown with a crown full of soft straight hair." Janai wanted to take it a step further. "Jordan, pick her up and put her in my arms for me."
Jordan looked at the nurse, then back at Janai.
"Please?"
He shook his head. He explained to Janai that she was hooked up to tubes and still fragile at the moment. He didn't even get to hold her earlier. The nurse overheard their conversation and decided that it would be okay for Janai to hold the baby for a few minutes.
The nurse took the child out of the incubator and placed her in Janai's arms.

When Janai held her daughter, she felt indescribable joy. She was overcome with emotions. Tears poured out of her eyes. She kissed her child and thanked God for giving her such a gift.

"She's precious, Jordan. So precious."

Jordan had tears in his eyes, too. He hadn't expected Janai to react like this. "I know, Janai, she's our precious little gem."

Just then the baby opened her eyes. Janai was tickled pink. The baby seemed to be taking everything in around her.

"I'm your mama and I love you. Do you know that? I'm going to protect you and make sure no harm ever comes your way. I'm going to be the mother to you that my mom wasn't."

Janai continued kissing and rocking her baby. Janai and Jordan decided it was time to name their child. Immediately, Janai wanted to name her Sapphire. She decided on that, because she was their precious little gem.

Jordan agreed. He loved it. He thought it fit her perfectly. He also suggested for a middle name that Janai use her grandmother's name, since she was one of the people she truly cared about and loved. Charmaine would be the middle name.

Janai smiled. "Sapphire Charmaine Johnson."

Jordan frowned. "You want her to be a 'Johnson' and not a 'Love'.

"No, that last name is bad karma. It has a stigma to it that I don't want for my child."

"You sure you want her to take my last name, even without knowing…"

She knew what he was getting at. She smiled softly. "I'll take my chances, J. In the meantime do you want to hold her?"

He took Sapphire from Janai's arms and smiled at her. He rocked her gently in his arms and nuzzled her close.

Janai liked the way Jordan was caring for the baby, even though he did not know for sure if she was his. Janai knew in her heart that Jordan was the sweetest and kindest man she had ever known and that he would make a fantastic father.

Janai was overcome with love for Jordan and Sapphire. She did not know what the future held for them, but one thing she knew for sure was that this was the most she'd ever loved anyone in her entire life and she wasn't going to blow it. She desperately wanted a family, this family.

Chapter 27

Chanel awoke to the smell of something delicious. When she got out of bed she reached for her silk kimono-style robe. Her black nightie was hanging on the doorknob reminding her of last night. She smiled, but that smile quickly faded when she realized that she was still unsure of her future with Donnell.

Chanel glanced at her hair in the mirror and hurriedly brushed it in place. She didn't want Donnell to see her in such a mess. She brushed her mane into a chignon securing it with hairpins. Chanel was now presentable enough to go downstairs to the kitchen to see what Donnell was cooking.

Donnell noticed Chanel walking down the corridor.
"Mornin', sleepy head."
"Good morning. What's going on?"
"What do you mean? I just wanted to make us some breakfast. You need to go shopping, by the way. Not much in there, but I managed to find some eggs and some cheese without mold on it."
They smiled at each other. "But, why now?"
"People change, Chanel. People change."
They sat in silence while they ate their gourmet-style omelets. Donnell finally broke the silence.
"Did you enjoy last night?"

Chanel blushed. "When have I ever *not* enjoyed sex with you?"

"Okay, I'll take that as a yes, but we both know it was more than sex." Suddenly she got uncomfortable and started squirming in her chair.

"What's wrong?"

"Nothing."

"Are you sure?"

"Yes, why?"

"I don't know. It just seemed like everything was fine until I mentioned us."

She faked a smile. "No, I'm cool." Chanel quickly finished her breakfast and headed for the shower. When she emerged from the shower, Chanel opened her closet door to find something to wear. Donnell came behind her and started kissing her on her neck. She shrugged him off.

"Donnell come on, I've got things to do today."

"I do too, but we can make time for each other, right?"

"No."

"No? What do you mean no?"

Chanel became upset and raised her voice at Donnell.

"Look all this is happening way too fast! I just need you to stop pushing me!"

Donnell was taken back a bit. "Chanel, you need to make up your mind. You tell me that you need time to think and the next minute you're standing in front of me in a sheer negligee. Then, we make love and you treat me as if I'm a stranger. Do you even know what you want?" He stormed out of her room.

Donnell was right. Chanel *was* confused. In the past she dove into her relationships heart-first. This time she wanted to take it slow and be sure to look before she leaped.

After spending two months in the hospital, Sapphire had gained four pounds and the physician thought she was healthy enough to finally go home. This was a big day for Janai in more ways than one. This was also the day that Janai would find out who fathered Sapphire.

Jordan walked in the room to find that Janai was breastfeeding Sapphire. He was amazed at how well Janai took to mothering.

"What a picture this would make," he said smiling broadly.

"Hi, J. As soon as I'm done feeding Sapphire we can go."

Janai noticed that Jordan was staring at her in a strange way.

"What?" she asked.

"I just got the results back from the paternity lab." They each had troubled and anxious looks on their faces. Waiting on the results to come back through the mail had seemed like an eternity. Jordan started at the envelope from Pro-Tech Labs Incorporated that came in the morning mail. It was marked CONFIDENTIAL. He sat down next to Janai and they both were holding their breath. Anticipation had them sitting on the edge of their seats.

The results came back and identified Jordan Johnson as having ninety-nine percent probability of being the father of Sapphire C. Johnson. Both Jordan and Janai breathed a sign of relief. They left the hospital to go home.

When the happy family pulled into Micki's driveway, they were greeted by a surprise. There was a big "Welcome Home" banner hanging across the front door. Both Micki and Chanel hugged Janai and grabbed for Sapphire.

"What's going on, Chanel?" Janai asked in bewilderment.

Chanel explained to her that since the baby had come sooner than anyone expected they never got a chance to throw her a baby shower. So she and Micki decided to do it upon her homecoming.

The girls instructed Janai and Jordan to go upstairs to her room and take a peek. Janai and Jordan slowly walked up the stairs to Janai's room and opened the door. The walls were decorated with pastel hues of pink, yellow, blue and red. There was also a crib with a Winnie-the-Pooh mobile hanging on it. Janai almost wanted to cry at the generosity of her friends. The two of them went back downstairs and noticed a stroller with a bow around it, and a few more items they thought she might need. There were undershirts and an economy size box of diapers, a swing, another car seat that can attach to a stroller, and some pajamas.

"How in the world did you guys find the time to do all of this?" Janai was touched by their love for her. Chanel and Micki both shrugged their shoulders. "We just did." Micki answered.

"I've got some great friends." Janai kissed her two friends, she felt blessed.

With all the commotion the baby started to cry. Janai placed Sapphire against her breast to feed her. Sapphire drank from her mother, then fell asleep.

Jordan watched in joyful silence as Janai's mother mode took over. He decided to leave once Janai put Sapphire down for a nap. He had some serious thinking to do.

One week after Chanel seduced Donnell, she decided to give him a call. She hadn't talked to him since that day. He answered the phone kind of short. "Yeah, hello?"

"Donnell?"

"Oh, hey Chanel, what's up?"

Chanel had made her decision and she was ready to see Donnell. She wanted to meet him at his place. Donnell was with a client, but he told her to meet him in an hour and a half.

When Chanel arrived at Donnell's place, he was on the phone. Chanel took off her coat, hat, and gloves. The winter weather had been brutal.

After Donnell finished his phone call he went to his bar to pour himself a shot of cognac.

"Chanel, do you want some?"

She shook her head. She needed to keep her mind unclouded. Donnell came and sat right next to Chanel on the couch. They were both face to face.

"So, what's up? What'd you want to talk to me about?"

"I think you know."

Donnell sat on the edge of the sofa.

"Donnell I've done some serious soul searching. I thought about everything we've been through and then, I thought about everything we could possibly go through…"

"And?"

"The last five years helped make me the woman I am today. I mean we had some really great times, Donnell, but there was more heartache than great times. At least for me anyway."

Donnell had a scowl on his face as he was listening to Chanel.

She also told him about the several times when her friends would tell her they saw Donnell out with different women. He would always lie and say that they were clients or he was just out with the guys. Chanel always felt in her heart that he hadn't been true to her.

Donnell shifted his weight. He did not like where the conversation was going.

Chanel continued. She told him that she chose to ignore her intuition. Big mistake. Even after all of that, she stayed because she was in love with Donnell. But the straw that broke the camel's back was when he brought that bitch into her home, into her bed.

"I still can't believe it." She was still hurting.

Donnell was extremely pissed off. He sat and flexed his jaw muscle, but didn't say a word. Chanel's demeanor seemed to change as she continued to talk.

"But then I started to see a man that I had never encountered before. I saw changes in you, Donnell that I never thought possible."

Donnell picked up his glass and sipped at his cognac and looked at Chanel with one eyebrow up. He wasn't sure which way the conversation was going. He couldn't read her.

"You finally poured your heart out to me. You told me that you loved me. And more importantly that, you showed me and I felt it."

"That's because I *do* love you."

"I know, Donnell, I know."

She knew that Donnell was truly sincere with how he felt towards her, but she just kept coming back to the same thing. She could not trust Donnell. How could she be in a marriage where she couldn't fully trust her husband? She looked Donnell in his eyes when she said this.

Donnell argued that within the last few months, he's shown Chanel how much he loves her, more than the entire five years they were together.

"Exactly Donnell, and that's just not good enough for me." Chanel wouldn't base a lifetime on something that's only been recently happening to her. She can only go by what she had been shown throughout the years.

"Chanel, what are you saying?" His voice cracked.
"I'm saying that as much as I love you, I can't marry you." She slowly pulled the sparkling marquis diamond ring off her third finger. She hesitated before giving it to him. Chanel had grown accustomed to wearing it.

Donnell couldn't even look at her. He just leaned back on the couch staring straight up, his eyes were misty. The only time Chanel had ever seen Donnell cry was when he lost his mother.

"You're not in love with me anymore?" Donnell whispered almost too softly to be heard.
"I love you, Donnell. I think there will always be a part of me that will always love you. But, that's not what this is all about. It's about me loving myself and learning what a healthy relationship should be based on."

Donnell shook his head. "I can't believe this. No...I don't accept this." He stood up and walked near the window. "Didn't the other night mean anything to you?"

"I have to go. I've said what I needed to say." She grabbed her purse and headed for the door.

"You didn't answer my question, Chanel. What about the other night? I felt something and I know you did too. Didn't it mean anything to you?"

Chanel had begun to feel a lump in her throat.

"If you can honestly tell me it didn't mean anything to you, I'll leave you alone, I won't bother you anymore."

This was harder than Chanel had anticipated. "It was just sex!" She screamed at him.

"Then I guess I don't know you like I thought I did."

His heart had been broken into one million pieces.

"Lock the door for me on your way out."

Once Chanel left, Donnell put his head in his hands and cried.

Janai, Jordan and Sapphire had started going to church with Micki regularly. Janai had become quite comfortable with this Sunday routine.

After church, Jordan would take Sapphire home with him so they could spend some quality time together. In addition to Sundays, Jordan also came by everyday after work and stayed until dinnertime.

That night, when Jordan returned Sapphire home, Janai held her close and rocked her baby in her arms. She felt blessed that her irresponsible behavior had not caused any permanent damage to her daughter. Janai stared down at her nursing baby and kissed her on the forehead.

"Do you know how much I love you? Please forgive me for hurting you. I've never loved anyone like this before." Janai had tears running down, she was overcome with emotion and love for her daughter.

"You're the best thing that ever happened to me. I promise I will never hurt you again." Janai nuzzled the sleeping Sapphire close to her. She put her in her bassinet and watched her as she slept.

The next afternoon Janai met Chanel for lunch at Applebee's. They sat and chatted and cooed at the baby, while their meals were being prepared.

"So, Micki tells me you've been going to church with her and everything. What's up with that?"

"I'm just trying some things differently, that's all. After all, I am a mother now." Janai smiled at Sapphire.

"Oh, my God! Are you alright?" Chanel checked Janai for a fever. They both laughed.

"No, it's just that up until I had her, my life was depressing. She has brought some positivity to my life. I just want to turn over a new leaf and start over."

"Dang! It's almost like you're a different person. She's really made you grow up, huh?" Chanel was surprised.

"Yeah. Speaking of changing, I notice you're not wearing Donnell's engagement ring anymore?"

Chanel's mood became sullen.

"No, I gave it back to him a couple of nights ago."

"What? Your one and only love?" Janai started to kid her, but instead offered her friend some comfort. "You alright?"

Chanel nodded. "I think so. I just had to do what was best for me you know," she said while stirring her tea.

Shortly after their meals, they were on their way back to Micki's place. Chanel decided to stay for a while and play with the baby until Jordan came for her. Micki left work early that day for some reason. She came in with some mail. She handed Janai her mail. Janai flipped through it without really having intentions on opening any of it until she noticed something with Clayton County Court division printed on it. She opened it and realized it was her worst nightmare.

"No!" She screamed at the top of her lungs and cried. "He can't do this!"

"Janai, calm down! What's wrong? You're scaring the baby."

Micki took the Sapphire upstairs and put her in her crib. Chanel took the paper from her and read it. Jordan was petitioning for full custody of Sapphire.

The petition stated that Janai was an unfit mother on the grounds of alcoholism, child endangerment, domestic violence and joblessness.

Janai went berserk! During all of this craziness Jordan pulled up. Janai saw him and ran out of the house and met him in the driveway. Micki ran after her to keep her from getting in Jordan's face. Janai made it to his car and started beating on it until Micki managed to pull her away just a little.
"What the hell is wrong with you, Janai?" Jordan screamed.

Janai told him he wouldn't get away with trying to take her daughter from her. She spat at Jordan, but it landed on his window. Jordan tried to explain. He didn't mean any harm; he just wanted the best for his child. Janai was becoming more hysterical by the minute. Jordan hit her below the belt and told her it was all her fault. If she hadn't been drinking while she was pregnant, none of this would be an issue.

Janai fell to her knees and cried. Jordan couldn't bear it. He *really* wasn't trying to hurt Janai. He just wanted the very best for his daughter.
Chanel could see the pained look on Jordan's face. She offered some advice.
"Look Jordan, why don't you give Janai some time to digest all this? I'm sure you two can work out something."

Jordan got back in his car and drove off. The music from the radio could not muffle Janai's wailing.

Chapter 28

For the first time since his mother's death, Donnell couldn't eat, or sleep. All he could do was think about Chanel and what could have been. He felt sick inside. He didn't know if he was coming or going.

Donnell was the type of man who was always prepared for anything, but he definitely wasn't prepared for that. Chanel had definitely blind-sided him. This was a time when he really needed his mother and he missed her more than anything now. He wished he could talk to her. Then he thought about calling his father, but he really needed a woman's point of view. So instead he called his Aunt Ruby, his mother's sister, who lived in Pasadena.

Aunt Ruby was the cool, hip aunt. She was a pleasant change from his strict and conservative parents. Aunt Ruby taught him lessons on the sly. Like the time when Donnell was twelve and he thought he was a man and wanted to try cigarettes. His aunt brought him in the house and let him light up one of her *"Kool cigarettes."* Although he choked when he took that first puff, she made him smoke the rest of it until he got sick. He hasn't touched a cigarette since.

Donnell picked up the phone and called his Aunt Ruby. Aunt Ruby answered the phone in her deep, husky voice that was caused by years of smoking and drinking.

Once they began speaking she knew right away that something was upsetting Donnell and that it involved a woman.

"How do you know all that Aunt Ruby?"

"Boy, I helped raise you. I kept your ass out of trouble. Hell, I was the one that gave you your first condom when you got your first piece of pussy."

Aunt Ruby had always been a card and she pulled no punches. All Donnell could do was laugh. He knew she was right.

"So talk to me, Donnell."

After a deep breath Donnell spilled his heart out to his favorite aunt.

His aunt felt his pain, but she also knew her nephew. She knew how much of a dog he had been in the past. He always had to have more than one woman, like he thought he was missing out on something.

Aunt Ruby told him that once a woman has been burned it's hard to regain her trust. And history always repeats itself, especially with men and their trifling ways.

Donnell got quiet.

"You don't have nothin' else to say, Donnell?"

"I just thought you were supposed to be on *my* side, Aunt Ruby."

"Boy, you know I keeps it real with you. I always have. And I'm not gon' stop now. Now I'm afraid you done blew it with miss Coco Chanel." His aunt always forgot the names of the girlfriends that Donnell had, so she used to make up nicknames for them.

"So you don't think that I can win her back at all?"

"No, not really. But if you try, just don't make an ass out of yourself. No woman want's a man who doesn't have at least some dignity. So don't be foolish and don't kiss her ass."

Donnell thanked his aunt for her advice. He knew that he had to do everything in his power to show Chanel that she was the one and only for him.

But how do I do that? He wondered.

Chapter 29

This was the day that Jordan and Janai would each appear in family court battling for the custody of Sapphire.

Janai was confident. She knew that the law was always on the mother's side. She also had support. Micki and Chanel had accompanied her. Jordan also had support. He had flown his mother down from Seattle.

Both Jordan and Janai were dressed conservatively. Jordan sported a navy blue suit with a crisp, white shirt and his head freshly shaved. Janai wore a long gray, pinstriped wool skirt with a soft, pink cashmere sweater.

Everyone in the courtroom was quiet when the judge entered. After a few formalities the hearing began.

"Mr. Johnson you have quite a few allegations about Ms. Love," stated the small Cuban judge. The judge put on his glasses to read the petition. "You are seeking custody on the grounds of alcoholism, child endangerment, domestic violence, and you also state that Ms. Love is jobless. Is all this correct?"
"Yes, your honor."
"Explain yourself."

Jordan went on to tell the judge that Sapphire was born prematurely which was in large part due to her mother's drinking.

Janai stared at Jordan in disgust. She couldn't believe he was airing their dirty laundry in public like this.

The judge nodded and shifted his eyes toward Janai. "Continue."

"I don't want my child to be exposed to such irresponsible behavior."

Janai was up in arms. "How dare you…." Before she could finish, Jordan's mother cut her off.

"You tramp, don't you ever get in my son's face."

"Another outburst from either of you and I'll hold you both in contempt of court. Go ahead, Mr. Johnson, you were saying?"

"Ah, yes well as you just witnessed she's a loose cannon and she's extremely violent. In the past she had struck me in the face several times and the most recent was when she learned I was taking her to court. I simply came to pick up my daughter and she ran outside to attack me. Her friends, who are also in the court room, witnessed the whole thing."

Chanel and Micki both gasped. They couldn't believe he would stoop so low as to try to use them against Janai.

Jordan also went on to say that he hadn't seen his daughter in several weeks, and that Janai does not have a stable home for their daughter nor does she have steady employment. Jordan has both.

"Very well, Mr. Johnson." Judge Santana turned toward Janai. "And just what do you have to say about what was just stated, Ms. Love?"

"He's just trying to spite me. He just wants to hurt me, because I broke up with him and he's still bitter about it."

Jordan chuckled. He couldn't believe she had said that.

Next the judge asked Janai a string of questions. They were in reference to employment and drinking.

Of course, she denied anything that would make her look bad in the courtroom. She felt she had no alternative, but to lie. She didn't want to lose her child. She even went so far as to tell the judge that she didn't let Jordan see Sapphire because she thought he would flee the country with her.

"Ms. Love, please spare me the dramatics. I wasn't born yesterday. Now one last thing, before I make my ruling. Is it true about your violent episodes?"

"No. Under no circumstances did I ever hit Jordan." The judge nodded. "Before I make my ruling, is there anything either of you have to say in your own defense?"

Janai raised her hand like she was in elementary school.

"I just want to say that I love my daughter so much and all I want is what's best for her and that is for her to remain with me. She's healthy and she's happy."

"So noted, Ms. Love…and what about you, Mr. Johnson? Any last words?"
"No, just some documents to back up what I have been saying."
The judge looked from underneath his glasses. "What kind of documents?"
Janai looked at Jordan and then back at the judge and seemed rather nervous. She couldn't imagine what he could have.

Jordan stated that he had the doctor's report showing that Sapphire had alcohol in her blood stream at birth.
Janai freaked out, her heart was beating rapidly.
Jordan also handed the bailiff a police log from the domestic dispute calls to 911.

"Let me review these documents." Judge Santana motioned for the bailiff to bring them over to him. " I will call a recess to review these in my chambers. Court will reconvene in thirty minutes." The judge banged his gavel and disappeared into his chambers.

Janai ran out of the courtroom and into the women's restroom to compose herself and to keep from saying anything to Jordan. Chanel and Micki followed her. She had splashed some water on her face and took a few deep breaths.

"Are you okay," Micki asked.
"Hell no! He's bringing up all that old shit. I'm a changed woman now. I'm not that person anymore."

A minute later Jordan's mother walked in. She stared Janai up and down. She was a short stout woman with a sharp tongue.

"My son should never have been with the likes of you anyway. When you lie down with dogs you wake up with fleas and I'm sure you gave him more than fleas."
"Old woman you better get out of my face." Janai was ready to fight.
Chanel jumped in front of the woman. Jordan's mother was ranting and raving and waving her hands every which way shouting obscenities. She called Janai all kinds of names. Then, she walked out of the restroom with her nose in the air.

When court was back in session, everyone took their places. Jordan and Janai both looked rather nervous. The judge had come from his chambers and took a seat. He began speaking.
"I love my job, but the one thing I hate is for children to be torn away from either parent. However painful, I must make a ruling, but it's only

239

a temporary ruling. We will then meet again in one month to re-assess. I rule that Jordan Johnson will take over the responsibility of full time parenting." Jordan and his mother jumped up for joy.
"Quiet!" The judge pounded his gavel.

Janai openly wept as the judge continued. He stated that Jordan can provide a more stable environment and this is a trial period for one month and they are to report back in such time. Janai was allowed unsupervised visits on the weekends only.

The judge turned to speak directly to Janai. "I don't feel as if Mr. Johnson is trying to spite you. I believe he truly loves his daughter. Custody will be granted to Mr. Johnson starting today at five PM. Ms. Love, please use this time to get your life together. Court is adjourned."

Jordan and his mother walked out of the courtroom. Janai was still in the chair sobbing. Micki and Chanel tried to comfort her, but it was no use. They helped her walk out to the car. When they got in the parking lot Jordan and his mother were out there. Janai walked up to Jordan.

"Janai stop!" Chanel thought she was going to attack Jordan.
"I'm okay. I'm not going to do anything crazy. I just want to talk to him." Janai looked at his mother.
"J, may I speak to you alone?"

"Anything you can say to my son, you can say in front of me," his mother interjected.

"Mama, please. Just get in the car and wait for me." She did, but not without cursing.

"J, why do you want to hurt me so bad? You know I don't act like that anymore."

"Janai, I *don't* know that. And I'm not trying to hurt you. This isn't even about you. It's about wanting my daughter to grow up in a stable environment. With positive people and a place where she can call home. If I truly thought that you had changed I wouldn't have gone through with it. I gotta go, Janai. Have my daughter ready by five. I won't be late." He walked off.

Janai didn't know what to say. She just walked back in the direction of her friends who were waiting for her inside the car.

Chapter 30

Janai hadn't been herself since the day Jordan was granted temporary custody of Sapphire. Although she was allowed to see Sapphire on weekends it wasn't the same, she still missed her baby girl.

All she did was mope around and cry. She was so stressed and upset that she would lose her child permanently that she had lost twenty pounds.

Micki knocked on Janai's bedroom door shortly after she had come home from church.

"What!" Janai yelled from the other side.

"Come downstairs for a minute. I want to talk to you."

"I'm not feeling well."

"Janai, I'll be downstairs whenever you're ready to talk." She knew that Janai wasn't sick at all. She had been in a mood for quite a while, though Janai did perk up when it was time to get her baby.

Janai walked downstairs a few minutes later. Her hair was all over her head with pieces of fuzz sticking out of it. She had on a t-shirt underneath a bathrobe and a grimy pair of socks and some multicolored wrinkled, dingy pajama bottoms.

"What is wrong with you, girl? Have you even showered today?" Micki was shocked by Janai's shagginess. "You look a mess. I've never seen you like this. The girl that once rocked *Gucci* and *Dolce and Gabbana* suddenly looks like a hobo on the street."

Janai didn't even have the energy to argue, she just shrugged her shoulders.

"Janai, you're just going to have to snap out of it. I mean I know you've been upset that you don't see your daughter on a regular basis, but you have to move on. You have to continue to have a life. You haven't even been job hunting during the week," Micki pointed out to Janai.

"Enough!" Janai raised up. "You don't know what the hell you're talking about, Micki. First of all, you're not a mother. And secondly, you couldn't imagine the pain I'm in right now." Janai felt defeated and hopeless.
Janai's outburst was the most emotion Micki had seen from her in weeks.

"I gave birth to the most precious baby in the world and I lost her. The judge thought so little of me that I basically lost my rights as a mother. Unfit! Then on top of that I feel guilty enough because I drank while I was pregnant." By this time, Janai was screaming at the top of her lungs.
"Do you know how that fucks with my head? My child may have severe health problems because of me. And I have to live with that for the rest of my

life. There's not a day that goes by that I don't think about it. So when you got that shit on your plate, then you come and talk to me."

"Look Janai, I'm sorry. I know I can't imagine what you're going through or what you're feeling, but all I'm saying is you gotta start taking responsibility for yourself and once you do that, taking care of Sapphire will come easy. But you need to get back out there and work and start making your own money again, and then find you a place to live for the both of you."

Janai became defensive and folded her arms. "Oh, so you kicking me out now? I mean are you trying to tell me something or what?"

"Janai, you can just stop, because that's not what I'm saying. If I had a problem with you living here, believe me you wouldn't be here. But the only way that judge is going to look at you differently is if you start presenting yourself in a different manner."

Janai slumped her body on the couch next to Micki.

"It's just not fair, Micki. It seems like since I've tried to change my life for the better, only bad things have happened to me."

"Things happen for a reason, Janai. Just continue to pray and be patient."

"That's all I've been doing. It's Sunday and I can't even see my daughter."

"Janai you know the only reason Jordan won't allow that, is because of that stunt you pulled on Thanksgiving."

Out of the goodness of his heart, Jordan split the day so that he would have Sapphire in the morning and Janai could have her in the afternoon. That way they both could spend time with her. When Jordan came to pick Sapphire up later that night, Janai wouldn't give her back. She kept Sapphire for two days. Chanel and Micki had to convince her to give the baby back to Jordan before he called the police on her. Eventually she gave the baby back, but now Jordan has decided to punish Janai for her foolish actions.

Micki's little pep talk was just what Janai needed. The next day she started job-hunting again. She had been on several interviews, but so far no one wanted to hire her.
On Christmas Eve she received a call from Jordan. Janai thought that he was calling to rub it in her face, the fact that she wasn't going to get to see her daughter. She almost picked a fight with Jordan. Actually, it turned out to be the contrary. Jordan was calling to invite Janai to spend Christmas Eve and Christmas day with Sapphire. He didn't trust her to be alone with Sapphire because of the stunt she pulled at Thanksgiving. But he felt that they were two grown adults and their daughter shouldn't

have to suffer because they had a few problems with each other.

Tears came to Janai's eyes and her spirits were lifted. She called Chanel to let her know that she wouldn't be spending Christmas dinner with her and her parents.

When Janai walked into Jordan's place she saw the Christmas tree lit up with all types of beautiful decorations. She figured his mother had done everything; it had a woman's touch. And she could smell the ham mixed with brown sugar and topped with pineapples. She could tell they were definitely going to feast.

"Here, Janai, let me take your bag, I'll put it in the other room. You can sleep in there, and I'll just give my mother my bed for the night."

"Where will you sleep, J?"
"I'm fine. I'll just sleep on the couch."
"Okay, thanks." Just as Janai was taking her coat off and trying to get comfortable, Jordan's mother walked out of the kitchen with a scowl on her face.

"I don't see why she should get the other room. Make *her* sleep on the couch."
Janai didn't say a word. She managed to ignore her rude comments.

"Mama, please," Jordan replied. His mother raised her nose high in the air and went back in the kitchen.

Jordan went to get Sapphire out of her crib so Janai could play with her. Surprisingly, Janai and Jordan were able to have a civil conversation together. Jordan hadn't seen Janai light up like that and have fun in quite a while. Her whole attitude had mellowed.

On Christmas day they all had a wonderful time. They opened gifts, listened to Christmas music and sat and talked and laughed. Even Jordan's mother seemed to chill out and just relax a little and stopped being so uptight.

Everything went so well on Christmas that Janai and Jordan were able to resume their old arrangements with the baby. Jordan's mother flew back to Seattle and things just seemed to fall right into place. Jordan had begun to let Janai stay overnight more often, however still in separate bedrooms.

Jordan, Janai and Sapphire brought in the New Year together. It was a warm intimate family celebration, just the three of them. They had a bottle of sparkling cider chilling in the fridge and some juice for the baby.

Sapphire had started to push up on her own and seemed to be scooting. The two played with Sapphire on the floor with a large blanket and once she was asleep they played cards, talked and listened to music.

Near midnight, Jordan went to the kitchen to get their chilled glasses and a nice bottle of sparkling cider. They turned the music off and decided to watch the annual Peach Drop on television. As the countdown was going on Jordan made a toast.

"This is to the most beautiful little girl in the world. Sapphire. You've given me a gift like no other. I never really knew the joy that I could experience from just one person, and so tiny at that." They both chuckled. "And Janai I also want to say I've really enjoyed becoming re-acquainted with you over the last couple of weeks.

They clinked their glasses at the rim and sipped the bubbly. "HAPPY NEW YEAR!"
The noise startled Sapphire awake. She started crying and Janai went into the kitchen to get one of her bottles. Jordan rocked and fed Sapphire. Sapphire fell asleep on his chest. After she had been asleep a short while, Jordan put her in her crib in the bedroom.

Shortly after being put down, Sapphire had begun crying again. This time Janai went and checked on her. She had already been fed, her diaper wasn't soiled and there was no sign of a fever. Janai and Jordan were both puzzled as to why their daughter kept crying.

"She's probably just cranky," Janai said. "She hasn't really had a nap all day."
"Well, just the same I'm calling the pediatrician." Jordan was able to have the physician paged. He called back within minutes. He told Jordan that if they checked everything out and it seemed as if nothing was really wrong to wait until morning. If her crying persisted he was instructed to bring her into the office the next day for an evaluation.

After some time had passed the baby finally drifted off to sleep, allowing her parents to get some rest of their own. At about four in the morning, Janai got up to use the bathroom, and got a glass of water, then checked on Sapphire. Janai didn't want to disturb her sleeping baby so she turned on the hall lights. Sapphire seemed unusually still. Janai quickly turned on the light in Sapphire's room and was astonished by what she saw.

Little Sapphire's face had turned blue. Janai grabbed her baby and began to scream. She ran to the phone and dialed 911 with the baby in her arms. Jordan jumped out of bed to see what was going on. Janai was already speaking with the operator.

"My baby, she…she's not breathing. Her face is blue, you gotta hurry before she dies."

Jordan stood in the doorway and heard the whole thing. He grabbed his baby and tried to perform infant CPR. Sapphire coughed and her color started returning. When the paramedics arrived they rushed the baby to the children's hospital downtown. Janai rode in the ambulance and Jordan followed in his truck.

"Oh, my God, please don't let her die." Janai prayed aloud.

The female paramedic touched Janai's arm to reassure her. "Don't worry, Ms. Love, she's going to be just fine."

Once they got inside the hospital the paramedics rushed Sapphire to the emergency room to be evaluated by a doctor.

"What's going to happen?" Jordan asked the doctor.

"We have to run a series of tests to see if there is normal brain activity, since she wasn't breathing."

Janai and Jordan both nodded.

The two frantic parents went into the waiting room. Jordan couldn't sit down and Janai kept crying. Jordan tried to console her. She cried on his shoulder.

"I'm a bad mother. That's why all of this is happening."

"What?" Jordan looked at her in a strange way. "Stop talking like that Janai, this was an accident." "No, I'm being punished for not treating her right while she was in my womb. And I never wanted her, J. Not at first. That's why I kept drinking."

He didn't want her to say another word. "Will you just stop it!" He yelled. "We got her here so she's in good hands, but we have to pray, Janai." He took her hands and they both bowed their heads and said a prayer for little Sapphire.

The doctor came out an hour later to let them know their daughter was fine, she had just developed an acute case of asthma. He told them they would have to use a nebulizer for her at bedtime.

Thank you, God!" They both said.

When Janai and Jordan returned home later that day with the baby, a neighbor knocked on their door and gave Jordan a piece of mail addressed from Pro-Tech Labs Inc.

"Here you go Jordan, that stupid mailman of ours keeps delivering your mail to my apartment."
"Oh, I appreciate it man."
Janai was sitting on the couch rocking the baby. She noticed the peculiar look on Jordan's face. "What's that, J?"
"I'm not sure. It's from Pro-Tech."

"Oh, it's probably just a bill."

Jordan shrugged his shoulders. He sat at the kitchen table and opened up the envelope. He was devastated by what he read. There had been a mix up with the names at the lab and the test actually revealed Jordan was not Sapphire's father. He slammed his fist onto the table and held his face in his hands. Janai jumped up and went to see what was going on.

"J, what's the matter?" she asked. Janai grabbed the piece of paper that had fallen to the floor and read it. Her heart dropped. Janai tried to touch Jordan, but he pulled away.

"Just leave me alone for a minute. I need a moment to gather my thoughts."

"Sure, I'll be in the back room."

A few hours later Jordan appeared in the doorway. He stood and listened to Janai talk to Sapphire. She looked up and became startled. "How long have you been standing there?"

"Not long."

"Look for what it's worth, I'm sorry about this whole mess I've caused. I'm sorry I endangered Sapphire's life, I'm sorry I hurt you, I'm sorry about how I've treated you in the past, when all you ever did was be a good man." She began to sob.

Jordan nodded. "I can accept all of that, but what I can't accept is this little girl being out of my life."

"What are you saying?"
"I'm Sapphire's father in every way that counts. My blood may not run through her veins, but we have a special bond. I couldn't leave that little girl if I tried. So I hope you will continue to let me see her, Janai."

"J, why would you even think I wouldn't allow you to see her?"
"I just thought with things being the way they are now that you would be getting full custody of her and I would get cut out the picture."
"Well, I won't tell the judge, but you have to drop the petition."
"Fair enough. We'll have to sit down and make the arrangements."
"We could switch off every week if you want." Janai offered.
"No, I'm talking about something more permanent, Janai." He took her hand. "I'm talking about you moving back in with me. Things have been going great between us and this little girl seems to have bridged the gap."
"Are you serious, J?"
Jordan smiled and picked up his little girl and rocked her back and forth.

Chapter 31

Chanel was busy painting her bathroom a shade of periwinkle. She had wanted to do it last summer, but just never got around to it.

She also got everything to match once it was finished. She got a pale pink waste basket with a matching shower curtain and liner, and she also got a seat/tank cover for the toilet that was periwinkle along with a rug, the toothbrush holder and soap dish. Then she topped it with some plastic flowers in pretty pastels to sit on top of the toilet.

As soon as she was finished, her doorbell rang. She was hot and perspiration had consumed her forehead and nose. She peeked out the window to see who it was. Donnell stood there looking as good as ever. She opened the door.

"Hi Chanel, I know this is out of the blue, but may I come in for a minute?"
She motioned for him to enter. He walked over to her couch and took a seat.
"You look busy."
"I was painting."
Donnell nodded. "Look Chanel, the reason why I'm here is because I think about you all the time. I love you and I know you love me, too."

"Donnell, why are you bringing this up now? We haven't spoken in months-since Thanksgiving."

"I have to try at least one more time, otherwise I might not ever know what could have been. I know you weren't being honest when you told me our last encounter was *just sex.*"

"Maybe not, but it doesn't even matter now. I've moved on with my life, and I thought by now you would have, too."

"Chanel, I'm going out on a limb, but I love you and I think you're worth it. I'm asking you to marry me again. Will you marry me?" This time he had a different ring. It was in a little blue box from *Tiffany's*.

"Say what, Donnell?"

"I'm not leaving until I get an answer. So what's it going to be?"

Chanel thought that Donnell had never been sexier than he was at that moment.

****

Their wedding was small but beautiful. There were at least fifty people in attendance. The groom's parents, family and friends sat on one side while the bride's friends sat on the other side of the small chapel.

On Valentines Day, Janai Love became Mrs. Jordan Johnson.

Jordan had proposed shortly after Janai moved back in the apartment with him. He saw changes in her that he never thought possible. She was an excellent mother and a dutiful girlfriend. He wanted them to remain a family.

Chanel held Sapphire in her lap during the ceremony. She couldn't help but think about Donnell's second marriage proposal. She still loved him, but wanted more than that in a relationship. She wanted someone to think that she was the most important person in the world. She knew she would never be that person for Donnell. She hadn't heard from him since she had turned him down, and she didn't expect to, either.

Janai was finally happy. She no longer needed other men in her life to make her feel worthwhile. She had Jordan, who loved her in spite of the turmoil she put him through. He was such a wonderful man and a loving father to Sapphire. She knew she was lucky to have him in her life.

Janai wanted to remember this special day forever. She assembled all her loved ones to take a picture with her. Janai couldn't help but smile when Micki and Chanel gathered on either side of her for the picture. These were the friends who stood by her during some extreme circumstances.

Malcolm is a wealthy virgin who decides to conceal his wealth
From the world until he meets the right woman. His wealthy best friend,
Dexter, hides his wealth from no one. Malcolm struggles to find love in an
environment where vanity and materialism are rampant, while Dexter is
getting more than enough of his share of women. Malcolm needs develop
self-esteem and confidence to meet the right woman and Dexter's
confidence is borderline arrogance.

Will bad boys like Dexter continue to take women for a ride?

Or Will nice guys like Malcolm continue to finish last?

Tina develops an insatiable sexual appetite very early in life. She only loves her boyfriend, Darren, but he's too far away in college to satisfy her sexual needs.

Tina decides to get buck wild away in college
Will her sexual trysts jeopardize the lives of the men in her life?

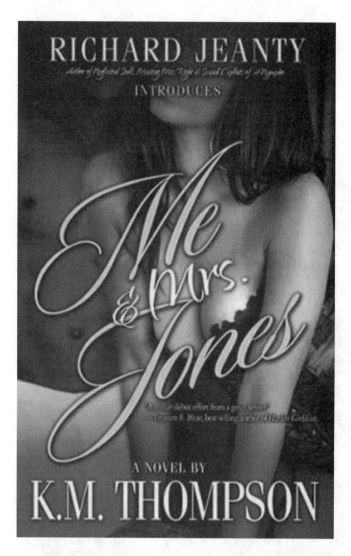

RICHARD JEANTY

Author of Boyfriend Dolls, Missing You, Trife ol Social Qolzers of A Hypocite

INTRODUCES

Me & Mrs. Jones

A NOVEL BY

K.M. THOMPSON

Faith Jones, a woman in her mid-thirties, has given up on ever finding love again until she met her son's best friend, Darius. Faith Jones is walking a thin line of betrayal against her son for the love of Darius. Will Faith allow her emotions to outweigh her common sense?

NEGLECTED SOULS
Richard Jeanty

Motherhood and the trials of loving too hard and not enough frame
this story...The realism of these characters will bring tears to your spirit as
you discover the hero in the villain you never saw coming...
Neglected Souls is a gritty, honest and heart stirring story of hope
and personal triumph set in the ghettos of Boston.

Neglected
NOMORE

THE SEQUEL TO *NEGLECTED SOULS*

RICHARD JEANTY

Jimmy and Nina continue to feel a void in their lives because they haven't a clue about their geneological make-up. Jimmy falls victims to a life threatening illness and only the right organ donor can save his life. Will the donor be the bridge to reconnect Jimmy and Nina to their biological family? Will Nina be the strength for her brother in his time of need? Will they ever find out what really happened to their mother? How will they handle the news about their mother? Will their grandparents Mr. and Mrs. Johnson have a change of heart about family situation? Find out as we explore the Johnson family further in the continuation of the struggle that Nina, Jimmy and the rest of the Johnson family have to face.

261

Betrayal, lust, lies, murder, deception, sex and tainted love frame this story... Julian Stevens lacks the ambition and freak ability that Miko looks for in a man, but she married him despite his flaws to spite an ex-boyfriend. When Miko least expects it, the old boyfriend shows up and ready to sweep her off her feet again. Suddenly the grass grows greener on the other side, but Miko is not an easily satisfied woman. She wants to have her cake and eat it too. While Miko's doing her own thing, Julian is determined to become everything Miko ever wanted in a man and more, but will he go to extreme lengths to prove he's worthy of Miko's love? Julian Stevens soon finds out that he's capable of being more than he could ever imagine as he embarks on a journey that will change his life forever.

RICHARD JEANTY

Author of *Rightand Daily, Meeting Mrs. Right & Sexual Exploits of A Nympho*

WARNING
HIGHLY
ADDICTIVE
READING MATERIAL

SEXUAL
exploits of a
NYMPHO
PART 2
"The Relapse"

Just when Darren thinks his relationship with Tina is flourishing, there is yet another hurdle on the road hindering their bliss. Tina saw a therapist for months to deal with her sexual addiction, but now Darren is wondering if she was ever treated completely. Darren has not been taking care of home and Tina's frustrated and agrees to a break-up with Darren. Will Darren lose Tina for good? Will Tina ever realize that Darren is the best man for her?

263

Ronald Murphy was a player all his life until he and his
best friend, Myles, met the women of their dreams during
a brief vacation in South Beach, Florida. Sexual Jeopardy
is story of trust, betrayal, forgiveness, friendship and
hope.

Order These Exciting Novels From

Available at bookstores everywhere

Use this coupon to order by mail

1. Neglected Souls (0976927713--$14.95)
2. Neglected No More (09769277--$14.95)
3. Sexual Exploits of Nympho (0976927721--$14.95)
4. Meeting Ms. Right(Whip Appeal) (0976927705-$14.95)
5. Me and Mrs. Jones (097692773X--$14.95)
6. Chasin' Satisfaction (0976927756--$14.95)
7. Extreme Circumstances (0976927764--$14.95)
8. The Most Dangerous Gang In America (Coming March 2007)
9. Sexual Exploits of a Nympho II (0976927772--$15.00) Coming Fall 2007
10. Sexual Jeopardy (0976927780--$14.95) Coming February 2008

Name_____

Address_____

City_____State_____Zip Code_____

Please send the novels that I have circled above.

Shipping and Handling $1.99
Total Number of Books_____
Total Amount Due_____

This offer is subject to change without notice.
Send check or money order (no cash or CODs) to:

RJ Publications
290 Dune Street
Far Rockaway, NY 11691

For more information please call 718-471-2926, or visit
www.rjpublications.com

Please allow 2-3 weeks for delivery.

Order These Exciting Novels From

Available at bookstores everywhere

Use this coupon to order by mail

1. Neglected Souls (0976927713--$14.95)
2. Neglected No More (09769277--$14.95)
3. Sexual Exploits of Nympho (0976927721--$14.95)
4. Meeting Ms. Right(Whip Appeal) (0976927705-$14.95)
5. Me and Mrs. Jones (097692773X--$14.95)
6. Chasin' Satisfaction (0976927756--$14.95)
7. Extreme Circumstances (0976927764--$14.95)
8. The Most Dangerous Gang In America (Coming March 2007)
9. Sexual Exploits of a Nympho II (0976927772--$15.00) Coming Fall 2007
10. Sexual Jeopardy (0976927780--$14.95) Coming February 2008

Name_____

Address_____

City_____State_____Zip Code_____

Please send the novels that I have circled above.

Shipping and Handling $1.99
Total Number of Books_____
Total Amount Due_____

This offer is subject to change without notice.
Send check or money order (no cash orCODs) to:

RJ Publications
290 Dune Street
Far Rockaway, NY 11691

For more information please call 718-471-2926, or visit
www.rjpublications.com

Please allow 2-3 weeks for delivery.

Order These Exciting Novels From

Available at bookstores everywhere

Use this coupon to order by mail

1. Neglected Souls (0976927713--$14.95)
2. Neglected No More (09769277--$14.95)
3. Sexual Exploits of Nympho (0976927721--$14.95)
4. Meeting Ms. Right(Whip Appeal) (0976927705-$14.95)
5. Me and Mrs. Jones (097692773X--$14.95)
6. Chasin' Satisfaction (0976927756--$14.95)
7. Extreme Circumstances (0976927764--$14.95)
8. The Most Dangerous Gang In America (Coming March 2007)
9. Sexual Exploits of a Nympho II (0976927772--$15.00) Coming Fall 2007
10. Sexual Jeopardy (0976927780--$14.95) Coming February 2008

Name_____

Address_____

City_____State_____Zip Code_____

Please send the novels that I have circled above.

Shipping and Handling $1.99
Total Number of Books_____
Total Amount Due_____

This offer is subject to change without notice.
Send check or money order (no cash orCODs) to:

RJ Publications
290 Dune Street
Far Rockaway, NY 11691

For more information please call 718-471-2926, or visit
www.rjpublications.com

Please allow 2-3 weeks for delivery.

Order These Exciting Novels From

Available at bookstores everywhere

Use this coupon to order by mail

1 Neglected Souls (0976927713--$14.95)
2 Neglected No More (09769277--$14.95)
3 Sexual Exploits of Nympho (0976927721--$14.95)
4 Meeting Ms. Right(Whip Appeal) (0976927705-$14.95)
5 Me and Mrs. Jones (097692773X--$14.95)
6 Chasin' Satisfaction (0976927756--$14.95)
7 Extreme Circumstances (0976927764--$14.95)
8 The Most Dangerous Gang In America (Coming March 2007)
9 Sexual Exploits of a Nympho II (0976927772--$15.00) Coming Fall 2007
10 Sexual Jeopardy (0976927780--$14.95) Coming February 2008

Name_____
Address_____
City_____State_____Zip Code_____

Please send the novels that I have circled above.

Shipping and Handling $1.99
Total Number of Books_____
Total Amount Due_____

This offer is subject to change without notice.
Send check or money order (no cash orCODs) to:

RJ Publications
290 Dune Street
Far Rockaway, NY 11691

For more information please call 718-471-2926, or visit
www.rjpublications.com

Please allow 2-3 weeks for delivery.

Order These Exciting Novels From

PUBLICATIONS
BRINGING EXCITEMENT, FUN AND JOY TO READING

Available at bookstores everywhere

Use this coupon to order by mail

1   Neglected Souls (0976927713--$14.95)
2   Neglected No More (09769277--$14.95)
3   Sexual Exploits of Nympho (0976927721--$14.95)
4   Meeting Ms. Right(Whip Appeal) (0976927705-$14.95)
5   Me and Mrs. Jones (097692773X--$14.95)
6   Chasin' Satisfaction (0976927756--$14.95)
7   Extreme Circumstances (0976927764--$14.95)
8   The Most Dangerous Gang In America (Coming March 2007)
9   Sexual Exploits of a Nympho II (0976927772--$15.00) Coming
    Fall 2007
10 Sexual Jeopardy (0976927780--$14.95) Coming February 2008

Name_____
Address_____
City_____State_____Zip Code_____

Please send the novels that I have circled above.

Shipping and Handling $1.99
Total Number of Books_____
Total Amount Due_____

This offer is subject to change without notice.
Send check or money order (no cash orCODs) to:

RJ Publications
290 Dune Street
Far Rockaway, NY 11691

For more information please call 718-471-2926, or visit
www.rjpublications.com

Please allow 2-3 weeks for delivery.

Order These Exciting Novels From

Available at bookstores everywhere

Use this coupon to order by mail

1. Neglected Souls (0976927713--$14.95)
2. Neglected No More (09769277--$14.95)
3. Sexual Exploits of Nympho (0976927721--$14.95)
4. Meeting Ms. Right(Whip Appeal) (0976927705-$14.95)
5. Me and Mrs. Jones (097692773X--$14.95)
6. Chasin' Satisfaction (0976927756--$14.95)
7. Extreme Circumstances (0976927764--$14.95)
8. The Most Dangerous Gang In America (Coming March 2007)
9. Sexual Exploits of a Nympho II (0976927772--$15.00) Coming Fall 2007
10. Sexual Jeopardy (0976927780--$14.95) Coming February 2008

Name_____

Address_____

City_____State_____Zip Code_____

Please send the novels that I have circled above.

Shipping and Handling $1.99
Total Number of Books_____
Total Amount Due_____

This offer is subject to change without notice.
Send check or money order (no cash orCODs) to:

RJ Publications
290 Dune Street
Far Rockaway, NY 11691

For more information please call 718-471-2926, or visit
www.rjpublications.com

Please allow 2-3 weeks for delivery.